WHEN MARY DIED

C.L. BELL

To

Tara,

From

C.L. Bell.

X

Published by Firouze Press

Copyright © CL Bell 2018

The right of CL Bell to be identified as author of this work
has been asserted in accordance with the Copyright,
Designs and Patents Act 1988.

British Library Cataloguing in Publication Data.
A CIP catalogue record for this book is available from the
British Library.

ISBN: 978-1-9996760-0-1

Dedication

Thank you to my husband for his unswerving
support.

Acknowledgements

Niki and Michael for being there.

Suzan Collins and the Waveney Authors Group
(without whom this book would never have been
written) for their guidance and help.

Nick Hedges photography (front cover)

INTRODUCTION

We all have layers. Layers that conceal our true identities. The more layers we peel away, the more we find. Some layers are good and pure and selfless whilst others hold a rottenness which festers like a silent plague just waiting...waiting...until it consumes the good and overtakes our thoughts and deeds. It is this rottenness that allows us to do evil things. We may lie, steal, cheat, fight or do other atrocities too awful for decent people to contemplate. Most of the time the rotten layers stay hidden, covered by the good layers and so the danger and evil is locked away in a deep dark area of ourselves. But there are people who cannot hide their rottenness. These are the folk we fear for they have no morals. They show no shame. They gloat and boast over the misdeeds they perform. They smile silently when thinking of their wickedness. They are uncontrollable and unstoppable. We all have layers. We live with these layers inside us.

As I stand here in the street, looking at the boarded up tenement building that was my home, I'm transported back in time to that awful Saturday. The Saturday that changed me. I had no conception as to how my life would proceed as the innocence of my childhood would be ripped from my heart. I would be left with a cynical fearsome maturity that was far beyond my eleven years. I remember. I remember it all.

I lived in a flat in a tenement building in the north east of Scotland. A normal, everyday, ordinary tenement which had three floors. Two flats on each floor housing normal ordinary folk. We shared a drying green at the back of the building with three other tenements which stood at right angles to our one. At the far end of the green was a long stone built shed. The women used it to hang their clothes inside on two ropes if the weather wasn't good. Our coal sheds stood along the other long side of the green.

We were a community. Everyone knew everyone else. Families were best friends with each other. Mothers sat in each other's kitchens drinking cups of tea and sharing local gossip. Fathers worked in the nearby factory together, went to football matches on a Saturday afternoon together and drank at the local pub after the game. In other words, we lived in each other's pockets. The children played in the back green when the weather permitted. They all went to the same school. If anyone had a problem, there was sure to be someone in the tenements who could help. If a family couldn't afford food, the others would rally round and make sure no one starved. Oh we weren't rich in the monetary sense, nothing like it, but we were rich in friendship and spirit.

Millionaires could have their large houses and estates with huge gardens, but we had our neighbours and friends. We were happy. We just didn't know how happy we were until…

CHAPTER 1

My eleventh birthday had passed a few weeks beforehand. I remember autumn arrived later than expected.

It was the middle of October and the warm weather disappeared as the night's became longer and colder.

I awoke that Saturday morning to the sound of muffled voices coming from the flat above. Mr. Milne was shouting at his son, Robbie, yet again. Robbie was sixteen years old but acted much younger.

"He had an accident and it hurt his brain", my mum told me when I remarked about his behaviour. Mrs. Milne had died a few years previously. I vaguely remembered her. She had nice hair and a lovely smile.

I lay in bed and tried to decipher what was being said above me, but I gave up after a while. A cold draught hit me as I sat up in bed. My curtains were slightly open and I saw a beautiful blue sky. I could smell coffee and toast and suddenly I felt hungry. My feet hit the freezing linoleum on my bedroom floor and I ran as quickly as I could to the kitchen.

"Well look who's up. It's little miss sleepyhead". My mum laughed. "It's half past eight. You've missed dad, he's gone fishing with Arthur next door. They won't be back until they're hungry I expect".

"When will that be?" I asked as I sat at the

pale yellow Formica table.

"About noon I'd say. I suppose the only thing they'll catch will be a cold". Mum turned and picked up my mug. "Here you are. Coffee. Do you want toast or cereal?"

"Toast please", I replied. "Mum, when I'm dressed can I go and see if Jean wants to come out and play?"

"Yes but you'll need to put on a jacket. It looks nice but its nippy outside". Mum looked out of the kitchen window. "So much for summertime then. Soon be snowing at this rate".
I finished my breakfast quickly. So quickly I got jam on my pyjamas. I went to get dressed and put on my scratchy woolly green jumper and my jeans.

"Can I go out now, mum?"

"Not yet, It's still a bit early. Amuse yourself whilst I get some work done in the kitchen".
I decided to play ice skating in our hallway. I could glide up and down and twirl in my socks and pretend to be a champion.

"Yoohoo it's only me". Mrs. Mclintock from across the lobby opened our front door. She wore her blue dressing gown and had pink curlers in her hair. "Oh look at you. Skating are you?"

Mum came out of the kitchen. "She thinks she's a gold medal winner. Mind you, last week she wanted to be a ballerina. I told her that if there's any cart horses in the Dying Swan, she'd get a part. What can I do for you Jeannie?"

"I'm clean out of sugar and the girls like to

have some on their cereal. Can I borrow some please? I'll get it back to you later today after I've been to the shops". Jeannie looked at me. "Oh I wish our Mary was your age still. I've just had such an argument with her".

Mum came out with a cup of sugar. "Why what's she done now?"

"She didn't like that skirt I made her. Said it's too young and only kids of our Jeans age would wear it. I could cry. I spent the good part of yesterday afternoon making it. I thought she'd love it. No, madam won't even try it on". Jeannie scowled. She was upset. "Mary was really cheeky as well".

"You'll need to put your foot down now. If you don't you'll regret it later". Mum looked at me, "I hope you're listening".

I nodded and carried on sliding. Mrs. Mclintock opened the front door and turned to me as she left, "Our Jean will be ready in half an hour. Just knock".

I couldn't wait. I was eager to get out into the sunshine.

As I kept sliding, I couldn't help but think of Mary. I wouldn't dare argue with my mum. I didn't like Mary much. She was fourteen years old, tall for her age everyone said. She had long dark red hair that hung to her waist and was shiny and she had big brown eyes. All the grown - ups thought she was beautiful. But being told that you're beautiful all the time had an effect, my mother once said. Mary had let it go to her head and she swanned around as if she owned the place. She didn't like the younger kids either. She bullied us. She teased me because I couldn't say my s properly. Mum said I had a lisp. And she bullied her sister, my best friend, Jean. She made Jean make her bed and do her chores when her mum, Jeannie, wasn't looking. Truth be told, we were frightened of Mary. I dreaded meeting her in the lobby.

"Can I go now?" I started to put on my green anorak.

"Yes, but stay in the back green. I've the broth and the trifle to make for dinner tomorrow so I'll be busy. Don't keep coming up". Mum shouted from the kitchen.

I shut the front door and felt the cold air of the lobby hit my cheeks. I knocked at the Mclintocks' door. Mary opened it. She looked prettier than ever.

"What do you want?" she snarled at me, "and what on earth are you wearing?"

"Is Jean ready? It's my anorak. It's my old one". I was wary.

"Jean your little friend is here. She's wearing a little kid's coat". Mary shouted.

I felt heat rise up to my cheeks. Mary stood and looked at me. What she said made me want to cry but I wouldn't, I just wouldn't. Jean came out. "Okay, I'm ready".

There were voices from the stairway. A man and a teenage boy came into view, followed by a woman who was panting as she tried to keep up with them.

"Hello young ladies", the man smiled at us,

"I'm Bill Strachan and this is my good wife, Marjory and our son Alex. We've just got the key to the upstairs flat, number six".

I smiled back at them. Mum would be pleased as she said she hoped it would be a nice family who moved into the flat on the top floor.

Mrs. McNab moved out two weeks previously to go and live with her son. She was old and couldn't manage the stairs anymore.

"Hello". I tried to sound friendly, "we're going out to play. I live over there", I pointed to our door, "and she lives in there". I nudged Jean. Mary stood in the doorway and twiddled her hair. She was smiling at Alex. He ignored her. Mrs. Mclintock came to the door.

"I thought I heard voices", she introduced herself.

Jean and I ran downstairs.

"So they're going to live in Mrs. McNab's house. I wonder if they'll like it. Mum said it needed a lot doing to it. Mrs. McNab had odd wallpaper". I turned to Jean. "Do you think they're friendly?"

I opened the back door. We went down the three steps onto the drying green.

"Have you got your skipping rope?" she asked.

I nodded. It was in my pocket. Just where I left it from the previous evening. We looked around.

Anita McKenzie was sitting on the bench outside the drying shed. She was Marys' best friend. They usually sat there and talked about film stars. Or boys. Or both.

If we went near to them, they would shout at us and tell us to get lost. Anita wasn't as bad as Mary, but she did as Mary told her.

When Mary wasn't around, Anita was nice and funny. But when Mary was there, Anita became nasty.

Mrs. Robertson, who lived in flat two on the bottom floor, came out. She nodded to us and went to her clothes rope. We watched as she hung her daughter Bunty's clothes out to dry. Bunty was twenty two and engaged to Brian. She worked in a local clothes shop. She was always dressed in a black skirt, white blouse and black cardigan. Bunty was tall with skinny legs. My dad said she looked like a spider. Mum said that was nasty. People couldn't help how they looked. Dad said they could at least try. Bunty dyed her hair blonde. Mum said that she fancied herself. I wasn't sure what that meant exactly but I knew it wasn't a good thing. Mrs. Robertson was a widow. Her husband died years before I was born. She was small and fat with grey hair in a bun at her neck. She was always complaining about Brian. Dad said that she didn't think he was good enough for Bunty and that only a millionaire would do for her daughter. But Bunty seemed happy with Brian. She shouted at him and bossed him around.

As Mrs. Robertson finished on the green, Brian appeared with his bicycle.

"I've got a puncture", he looked at Mrs. Robertson who was doing a good job of ignoring him. "I'll have to fix it here. Hello girls", he winked at us and we giggled.

Mrs. Robertson finished hanging the clothes and walked past. Brian pulled a face and we giggled again. I nudged Jean.

Anita had obviously seen Brian and was walking over to us. Brian started fixing his puncture. He was too busy to notice her.

"Is Mary nearly ready?" she looked at Brian but didn't say a word to him. Jean shrugged. Anita walked to the steps. "I'll go and see".

Jean and I had seen this happen before. Mary liked Brian. She would stand next to him and watch him mend the puncture, all the while smiling and asking stupid questions.

If Bunty came out, there would be an argument. Bunty didn't like Mary at all. Brian started to work on the bicycle. We walked to the middle of the green and I took out my rope. I noticed that Bunty had come out to talk to him.

"Oh I hope Mary doesn't come down now". Jean was worried. "She annoyed Bunty on Thursday and Bunty had a right go back at her. Mum had to apologise for Marys' behaviour. Dad was fuming".

"Why, what was it all about?"

"Mary said that Bunty had a cheap engagement ring and that Brian was poor. And that when she got married, Mary that is, she would have a big diamond ring and marry someone who could afford to have a car and not a stupid bike". Jean explained. "Bunty was furious. She shouted at Mary. It was awful".

"Oh", I couldn't believe that Mary would be

so horrid. "did your mum get really angry?"

"She shouted at Mary and slapped her. Mary was crying and said she hated mum and dad and me and everyone. She said she would be rich and famous and she'd show us all. We were stupid and she was too pretty to live here. She didn't want to waste her life with us. Mum was really upset. Dad didn't say anything but you could see he was angry". Jean looked over again. Mary had appeared on the steps with Anita in tow.

Bunty's brow was furrowed as she glared at her, and Mary made a beeline for Brian. We knew there would be trouble.

"Hiya", she shouted "what are you doing? Do you want me to help you? You know I will". Bunty walked up to her. "Leave him alone little girl. Why would he need you to help when he's perfectly capable of doing it himself? Go and play with your little pals. I bet you love playing skipping don't you?"

Marys' face turned red. She didn't answer, she just walked to the drying shed with Anita following behind.

"She's just a kid. She didn't mean anything. She just wanted to see what I was doing". Brian seemed angry with Bunty.

Bunty stamped her foot. "Maybe you don't know what she's up to, but I do. She's just trying to annoy me". She turned and walked inside.

"Women!" exclaimed Brian and ran after her. We heard her shouting at him. Jean and I didn't know what to do. Should we go and see if Mary was okay? Or should we just carry on playing. We decided to carry on as if nothing had happened.

"I'll get into trouble later", Jean looked sad, "every time Mary has an argument, she takes it out on me. She can be horrible".

"She'll forget by dinnertime". I felt sorry for Jean, "It'll be okay. You'll see".

But Jean was adamant. "No she won't. I have to share a bedroom with her. She cut my hair once and told mum I'd done it. I got into trouble. All because I used her hairbrush. I wish I was you. No sister to be awful to you".

"You should have told your mum". I was appalled.

"No. It would have made things worse. I'm a bit scared of Mary. She doesn't forget anything". Jean said.

Mary was sitting giggling with Anita. They ignored us, at least for the time being.
We played for a while. Then I heard a cough. I looked round.

Bunty stood at the back stairs. She was wearing a blue skirt that had lace round the hem. It was beautiful, and she knew it. With a pale blue blouse and white shoes, she looked quite pretty. She smiled at us.

"We're going into town, I came to see if the clothes were dry yet". She made her way to the clothes rope. "Do you like my new skirt? It came in to the shop yesterday. The other assistant liked it, but I managed to buy it before she could. She was a bit put out, but I always say that if you don't act fast, you won't get". She laughed.

I nodded and Jean said; "It's beautiful. Like something a princess would wear".

This pleased Bunty. The shouting, nasty Bunty had disappeared and in its' place was a nice, friendly Bunty. I wasn't sure. I thought that it wouldn't take much for the horrid Bunty to return. However, Brian shouted that he was waiting for her and he had her coat so she left. Jean and I breathed a sigh of relief. We could see that Mary was fuming. I didn't want to play skipping, so while we tried to decide what to do, Jean and I sat on the steps.

"Oh it's the young ladies", Mr. Strachan, his wife and son stood behind us. We moved aside and let them pass.

"What a lovely drying green. And look, is that a drying shed? Oh that's great. The coal sheds have numbers on them. What number is ours? Is it the same as the flat do you think?" Mrs. Strachan was very happy with the strangest things. "Yes it is. Bill, come and see, this is our coal shed".

Mr. Strachan smiled as he went over to the shed. Alex stayed with us. He lit a cigarette. It smelled awful. Only adults smoked, or so I thought. Alex saw me staring at him.

"You don't smoke?" he said. "I bet you're thinking that I shouldn't either. You're right, but I can't seem to stop. Not that I've tried very hard".

"My dad says it's bad to smoke. He doesn't.

Nor does mum. Dad says you might as well burn your money because that's all you're really doing".

He laughed. "Well I'm eighteen and I'm old enough to know better".

Mary had seen Alex and walked up to us.

"We're going to the shop. Want to come along?"

Mrs. Strachan had left the shed and was next to us now. "Sorry love, he's coming with me. We're going to get paint for the living room", she turned to Alex. "Dad's going to get some biscuits and tea. You come with me. I can't carry heavy tins of paint. Come on now".

Mary was not impressed. She whispered but just loudly enough for Alex to hear, "mummy's boy, mummy says jump and he does. Mummy's boy. Mummy's little baby boy".

Alex said nothing but I could see he was mad. Mary walked away. She sat down once more on the bench by the drying shed. I could see her telling Anita what had happened. Then she laughed. Loudly.

"He wasn't happy". I looked at Jean. "Mary was awful. He was only helping his mum".

Jean shrugged. "She'll tease him about that now. She won't let him forget it. She thinks she's so grown up, but she's not. I hate her sometimes".

I knew what she meant. Mary was like a dog with a bone. She couldn't leave things alone.

She had to go on and on until people lost their temper with her. Then she'd run to her mum and dad and say nasty things about the person she's teased. Unfortunately they believed her.

Mum said that she always got away with things because she was so pretty and adults wouldn't believe that she could be horrid. Mary also loved to boast about what she'd done to annoy people. She took a delight in telling Anita. It was as if she enjoyed making people angry. Anyway, I was glad that I didn't have to live with her. I felt sorry for Jean. She was stuck with Mary.

I didn't want to think about it anymore, so I told Jean "I want to play chase", and we ran around laughing.

The dramas of the morning were soon forgotten. Mary and Anita left to go to the shop. We made a lot of noise. We played skipping happily together. None of the other children from the adjoining tenements came to play. Saturday morning was the usual time when they went shopping with their mothers.

The sun shone although there was a cool under current in the air. An odd feeling of something to come but not knowing what it was. I often thought about that morning. How things were obvious but only after the event. As the day unfolded I later wondered if any of us could have halted what happened. Of course we couldn't. No one could have foreseen the darkness that would descend and change us all forever.

CHAPTER 2

Sometimes we do things that can affect how we react to situations. If we start the day feeling happy and contented, the chances are that we'll feel the same way for the rest of the day. But if something happens to make us feel bad, if we 'get out of bed on the wrong side' then we can be upset until we go back to bed again. Little things will seem huge. Feelings will escalate until we want to explode. Situations can get out of control quickly and cause problems which might never be forgotten nor forgiven.

At one o'clock mum called me for my dinner. Jean and Mary went to have theirs as well. Anita returned to her tenement which was next to ours. She lived in the bottom right hand flat.

Dad was back. Mum was right. He hadn't caught any fish. He was in the bedroom getting ready to go to the football match. Dad and Arthur Mclintock always went to the local match together.

I sat opposite mum at the kitchen table and we started to eat our mince and potatoes. I was really hungry. Dad came in and winked at me.

"I'll away now. I'll get a pie and a cup of tea at the match. It should end around half past four. You girls be good now. Don't get up to any mischief". He smiled at us.

Mum looked up from her food, "It's sausage, egg and beans for tea. I'll have it ready for you. I suppose you and Arthur will be going to the pub

18

tonight".

Dad nodded. "Yes after teatime". He kissed us both on our heads and left.

Mum asked me about my morning. I told her about Mary and Bunty, Mary and Brian, Bunty and Brian and finally Mary and Alex. Mum listened and sat back in her chair. She sighed.

"Mary wanted the new boy, Alex to go to the shop with her and Anita. When he wouldn't, she called him a mummy's boy and a baby. She was scary. She was really scary this morning. Why is she like that mum?"

Mum looked serious. "Mary's at that age where she thinks she's older than she is. She thinks she knows it all and she just wants to argue all the time. It happens to some girls. Other girls are fine, but some girls find growing up confusing. The problem is, that Mary is very pretty and boys like that. If she's not careful she'll find herself in deep trouble before she's sixteen".

I wondered what trouble she'd get into. The boy who worked in the butcher shop got into trouble for selling sausages at the local pub. And John Michie in my class got into trouble for throwing stones and breaking Mrs. Bruce's window. I couldn't see Mary doing either of these things. Nor could I see her robbing a bank or a house. I was puzzled.

"What trouble?" I asked mum.

She stood up and put the plates into the sink.

"Girls like Mary are two a penny. They use their good looks to get boys interested in them.

They like to make other girls jealous and boast about it. It never ends well".

"Oh right". I was still puzzled but mum had turned away so I left the subject alone. I'd ask dad later.

There was a knock at the door. Mum answered and Jean came into the kitchen. I noticed that her eyes were red and she'd been crying.

"What's wrong?" I didn't like to see my best friend upset.

"Mary. She was in a bad mood about this morning and then she argued with mum. Mum called her a brat. I went into the bedroom. They were really shouting. Dad had left and I was scared".

I nodded. Mary could shout loud but Jeannie could shout louder. Jean went on. "Mary came into the bedroom. She told me to leave and hit me hard on my back. Mum was mad because dad came back from fishing and after a while got changed to go to the match. Mum wanted him to look at the iron because it's not working properly. He didn't and she was already mad. Then Mary started going on about her skirt and how she hated it. It was awful".

"Have you had any dinner, Jean?" Mum asked. Jean shook her head. Mum gave her a plate of mince and potatoes and said she'd talk to Jeannie later. Every problem seemed to come from Mary. I was sorry for Jean but thankful that I didn't have to live in a house where people argued most of the time.

After Jean had dinner, we went downstairs to play again. It was still cold, but we didn't care. Mrs. Bruce who lived in the other ground floor flat, always had her two grandsons visit on Saturday afternoon. Jean and I liked the boys. Peter was twelve years old and quite big for his age. Billy was eight and much quieter. They came out as we stood on the green. We all decided to play chase. Running around, no one saw Mary come downstairs and stand watching us. Peter chased Billy who bumped into Mary.

"Stupid little boy! Watch where you're going! You could have knocked me over you idiot!" Mary was fuming. She grabbed Billy by the shoulders and shook him hard. He started crying. Peter stepped in. He shouted at her.

"Oi, you, leave my brother alone", he pushed her away, "come on Bill, you're okay now. I'm here".

Mary was red with rage. "How dare you push me! He's nothing but a little cry baby who needs his brother to fight his battles. Huh, cry-baby bunting", she taunted him.

"Shut up!" Peter shouted clenching his fists. He was mad. "You're just a stupid girl!"
Mary kept repeating it and Billy cried louder. Mrs. Bruce had heard the noise and came out to see what was going on.

"Peter, take Billy inside. As for you madam, you're old enough to know better. You watch your step. One day all this nastiness will catch up with you and you'll get a shock". She went inside with the boys.

21

Mary turned away. Anita had returned and was waiting by the shed. Jean and I stood there, unsure what to do. If we said something, it would make matters worse, but if we didn't, Mary might shout at us. We tried to creep away as best as we could. We felt relief when Mary walked toward Anita. They sat on the bench and Mary started waving her arms around.

"She's telling Anita", said Jean. "I bet she lies about everything".

I thought about what mum told me one day when I was in a bad mood. She said that the mood would carry on for the rest of the day. Mary had argued with her mum at breakfast time and I supposed that the feeling was still inside her. Each argument was worse than the last one. Mum called it a chain reaction. I could see that was true. If Mary had only liked the skirt, then she wouldn't be in a bad mood. Jean broke my thoughts.

"We'll stay up at this end of the green. I don't want Mary to start shouting at me".

I agreed. Peter and Billy came out again. The minute that Mary saw them, she pointed and laughed.

"Ignore her". Peter told Billy, "She's just trying to upset you again. Don't let her get to you. She wants you to cry. It pleases her to be nasty like that. She's a bully. Come on let's play".

We carried on talking and eventually Mary gave up. I couldn't figure out why she was being so awful.

Mr. Milne and his son Robbie came past us and went to their coal shed. Robbie carried his yoyo. He always played with it.

"It keeps him calm and quiet". Mum told me when I asked why he always had it.

Mr. Milne opened the coal shed and began to fill his bucket. Robbie started to walk around the green. He played with the toy and sang Humpty Dumpty. As he approached Mary and Anita, he dropped the yoyo. Mary sprang up and grabbed the toy. She held it out. Robbie went to take it and she pulled it away, giggling to herself. She did this a few times. "Come on Robbie, try and get it".

Robbie let out a scream. A piercing scream. Then he started hitting his own head. Mr. Milne ran across to his son.

"What are you playing at?" He shouted at Mary. "You see what you've done? He'll take ages to calm down now. You evil little cow!"
Mary took a step back and threw the yoyo at Robbie

"I was only playing. I didn't mean anything bad. Honestly". She looked at Mr. Milne. "Anyway, it's just a stupid yoyo".
Mr. Milne looked as if he wanted to slap Mary. Jean and I were terrified. Jean said it was a good job Bunty wasn't there or she would have hit Mary. Bunty sometimes helped Mr. Milne with Robbie. She liked Robbie. Jean ran upstairs to get her mum. Mary didn't move.

Robbie had stopped hitting himself but he was still screaming. Eventually, Robbie calmed down. Jeannie had arrived on the green and went over to Mr. Milne.

"I'm so sorry for this". Her voice trembled. She was upset. "I don't know what's got into her. She's been horrible all day". She turned to Mary. "You, upstairs! March! You're for it now!"

Mary was having none of it. "I didn't do anything. I was playing. I didn't know he'd start screaming like that, did I? It's not my fault he's like that, is it?"

Jean stood beside me and fidgeted. "I'm going to get it now. I shouldn't have told on her. I'm silly. I'm really scared".

Mrs. Mclintock was now shouting at Mary who was trying to talk her way out of the trouble. But Jeannie was having none of it. Mr. Mine took Robbie over to the coal shed, locked the door and they both went upstairs. Finally, Mary and Jeannie followed, but not before Mary passed us and hissed at Jean, "I'll get you for telling on me".

Jean was shaking. I tried to reassure her. I said that she should tell her mum if Mary tried anything. Jean shook her head. She said it would make things worse. I gave her a hug. I hated seeing my best friend upset.

"Come on, we'll play skipping for a while. If you're really scared, maybe mum'll let you stay at ours for tea. Mary might be okay later on".

We played for a while. Skipping was our favourite game. Mary came out but ignored us and went back to the bench. Anita was still there.

We didn't care. We were having fun.

Alex appeared at the back door. He lit a cigarette and watched us. Mary saw him. She shouted.

"Oh look. It's mummy's boy. Hey mummy's boy, where's your mummy then?"

Alex ignored her. She kept on shouting. He turned to us.

"How come she's so pretty but she's really horrible? Has she always been like that?"

Jean thought for a minute. "No, she was okay before. She was funny and she laughed a lot. But in February our granny died. Mary used to go and stay with her on Fridays and I didn't care because I had mum and dad to myself. But when granny died, Mary changed. Mum said it was that but she also said a lot had to do with her age. Fourteen isn't an easy age mum said and Mary was changing".

Alex shook his head. "She's going to get into a lot of trouble if she keeps this up. Your mum needs to have a long talk with her. Anyway, I'm away upstairs to paint the living room. See you two ladies later".

He winked at us and we giggled. He was nice, for a boy. I thought the whole family were okay. Jean nudged me.

"Our Mary's mad again. Look at her face. She doesn't like being ignored".

Mary certainly looked grim. I wondered what she was thinking. Peter and Billy came out and Billy started running around. He stumbled and cut his knee. He started to cry.

"Aw look at him. The cry baby. Did you hurt

your knee cry baby?" Mary laughed and teased him.

Peter helped his brother up and took him inside. Mary laughed loudly but it was a fake laugh. Jean saw that I was angry. "Come on, just ignore her. She couldn't get Alex to answer her so she's trying to get Peter to have an argument".

I was happy to go along with that. My head was full of playing and skipping games. It would soon be tea time and I wanted to cram in as much playtime as I could.

Bunty and Brian returned. They came over to us. Bunty had a huge smile on her face. "Look what Brian bought me.

We didn't go to the cinema, we went to the shops instead. Look, at this". Bunty touched a locket which hung around her neck.
Jean and I were enthralled our eyes huge with wonder. A real gold locket shaped like a heart! It was beautiful. Out of the corner of my eye, I saw Mary walk toward us. I knew there would be trouble.

"Look Mary, Brian bought me a locket". Bunty was showing off.

Mary looked at it. "Is that it? Small isn't it. I would have had a much bigger one".

Bunty turned red but she kept smiling. "Well at least I have a man to buy me things. That's what happens when you're grown up. Of course, Mary, you won't know that. You're still a child". Mary glared at her but said nothing. Bunty turned to Brian and suggested that they go inside for some tea.

We waited for the storm to hit. It never came. Mary walked away and stood by the stairs. Jean and I were happy. "Thank goodness nothing happened then". I sighed with relief. I was glad that Bunty hadn't heard about Mary teasing Robbie as there was no telling what she'd do. Bunty really didn't like Mary.

Peter came out again. This time he had a football. He started to kick it against the wall. Unfortunately it was the wall outside Mrs. Robertson's flat. Within minutes, Bunty came out.

"What do you think you're doing? You aren't supposed to play football here. If you kick that ball and hit my clothes, I'll make sure you never kick it again". She turned to Mary "And what are you smirking at madam?"

Mary said nothing. She kept on smirking. Peter stopped kicking the ball. Bunty went over to the clothes. They still weren't dry. She unpegged them and walked down the green into the drying shed.

"I've left the clothes in there to dry. I'll get them later". She turned to Peter. "At least they won't get stained by a football hitting them".

I wouldn't be going anywhere near the shed. There was a stool at one end where people put their wash baskets and pegs, but at the other end, on the floor, was an old sheet. It had been there for ages.

It scared me. I shook every time I saw it. Mum said it belonged to someone in the other flats.

I knew that was true, but I imagined it was a ghost, just lying there waiting for the dark to fall and it would rise up and grab anyone who went into the shed. Mum said I had too much imagination and that's what I got from reading so many books but I was convinced that the sheet was a sleeping ghost so I avoided the drying shed as much as possible.

Bunty stared at Peter. Peter turned red and picked up the ball. Bunty walked past Mary and into the lobby. No one spoke for a while. We all stood there trying to look as if we were deciding what to do, but really scared to make a move. Then Mrs. Bruce came to the steps. She had a small bag in her hand.

"I forgot that I had these sweets. Peter, take them and make sure you share them out".

Peter took them and offered each of us a sweet. Strawberry bonbons. Mary stood watching. Anita came over.

"Hey Anita, would you like a sweet? Granny said to share them. Here you are".

He held out the bag and she took one, but he ignored Mary who was still looking on.

"What about Mary?" I asked. "Mary would you like a sweet?"

Peter scowled at me, but I was adamant.

"Erm yes please", Mary said quietly.

Peter handed me the bag and I held it out to her. She smiled and took a sweet. "Thanks. They're my favourites". She said.

I smiled back at her. She was like the old

Mary. The Mary who used to sing songs with us. The Mary who played skipping with us and told us stories. And I had to admit, when she smiled, she was very beautiful.

"Come on, let's go and see if I can go to your flat for tea". Mary said to Anita. She turned to Jean.

"And don't you go blabbing to mum. If Anita's mum says yes, then I'll go and ask mum myself. I don't need you to go tattle telling. Okay?"

Jean nodded and we watched as the two girls disappeared into the other tenement.

Peter looked at me. "I wouldn't have given her a sweet. She was horrible to our Billy. I would have ignored her. She didn't deserve one".

I shook my head. "That wouldn't be right. Anyway, she's just having a bad day isn't she? We all have them. I felt awful last Thursday. I got out of bed on the wrong side, mum said and I was crabby all day. I fell out with mum because I couldn't find my homework book and when mum told me that I'd left it in the living room, I huffed and puffed and felt mad. Then I fell out with Morag Miner in my class because she used my pencil without asking. She was wrong, but I was really horrible about it. That's what the matter is with Mary. She fell out with Jeannie this morning and now she thinks that the whole day is wrong".

"You're wrong", Peter was stubborn if nothing else. "she's just horrid. Anyway, we have to go home soon. Granny's coming to ours for her tea. Mum says we're having fish and chips tonight. What are you having?"

"We're having egg, sausage and beans. What are you having Jean?" I wondered if Jeannie would let Jean have her tea at ours.
There would be plenty. Mum usually cooked lots of sausages, well eight at least.

"Mum said we're having chips and egg. I think I should stay at home if Mary's going to Anita's". Jean smiled.
At that moment, Mary and Anita came out of the tenement and made their way to our building.

"Are you going to ask mum? Did Anita's mum say yes?" Jean was curious.

"Yes I'm going to ask her. And you better not snitch anymore or I'll get you back". The nice Mary had gone.
We watched as the two girls disappeared inside.

"I hope mum says yes. I don't want to sit and listen to mum and Mary arguing again". Jean was nervous. I could see that she really hoped that Mary would be going out for her tea.

Quite a few minutes later, Mary and Anita returned. Mary didn't say anything. She went and sat by the shed. Anita whispered to us.

"Mary and her mum had a bit of an argument. Jeannie said Mary should be back at seven o'clock. Mary said she was older now and wanted to stay at mine until eight o'clock. I thought Jeannie was going to say she couldn't come. Jeannie said Mary had to be back at the time she was given 'cause it gets dark between half past six and quarter to seven and, if she argued any more, she wouldn't be allowed to come for tea, ever! Mary isn't happy but at least she's coming".

Jean was pleased. Mary wouldn't be in the house for a while. There would be peace.

We played cowboys and Indians until Mrs. Bruce came to get Peter and Billy.

Mum shouted from the bedroom window. "I'm having a cup of tea with Jeannie. You have ten minutes to play then you'll need to come upstairs. Jean, your mum says the same. Remember now, ten minutes. I'll give you both a shout".

Brian walked towards us. He took his bicycle which was next to the steps. "Well girls, I'm away home now. Bunty and I are going out tonight. I better go home and get changed. You know how women are".

Jean was nosey. "Where are you going? Are you going to that dance at Nevis Hall? I saw something about it in the sweet shop. There was a poster with a man and woman dancing. I told my mum".

"No, we're going to the pictures. There's a film that Bunty wants to see. I'll have to get my skates on. My mum will have the tea on now. I need to be back here about quarter to eight. The film starts at half past. Don't you girls get up to any mischief. Brian lifted his bicycle up the steps and left.

Minutes later Mrs. Robertson came to the top of the steps. She looked around. "Did Bunty hang the clothes in the shed?" she asked me.

"Yes, they're there". I pointed.

"Okay. I'll just leave them then. She can take them in later before she goes out. I'll be at the bingo". She went inside.

We were happy. We played for a while and then mum called us.

I'd been playing for most of the day. Although the sun was still shining, the temperature had dropped, it felt cold and I started to shiver. I don't know why I did what I did next.

Before I went up the steps and into the lobby, I turned round and looked at Mary and Anita.

I waved to them both. "See you tomorrow".

Anita waved back and she and Mary started to walk towards the other tenement. I stood and watched as they went inside.

Little did I know that it was to be the last time I saw Mary alive.

CHAPTER 3

It was five o'clock as I walked through our front door. I heard the clock in the living room chime. Mum was waiting for me. She came out of the kitchen.

"Take your coat off and hang it in the cupboard. Your slippers are in your bedroom, oh and wash your hands. I'll sort the tea now. It'll be ready in a few minutes. Dad'll be back soon. I wonder how the match went".

I did as I was told. It took a while for me to wash my hands. They were filthy. We sat at the kitchen table. I was still wondering about what she'd said, about trouble and Mary. Other people had said the same thing. I was about to ask again when dad came in.

"Did you have a good time?" mum asked him. "We've just sat down. I'll put your tea out now". Dad frowned and said he didn't know why he bothered to support the team. Once again they were rubbish! He went to the bathroom. When he returned he sat opposite me. I waited for a while but I couldn't keep it in any longer.

"Dad, mum says Mary had better watch out or she'll get into trouble. What trouble is it?" Dad stopped eating and glanced at mum. She coughed. He looked at me and sighed. "Nothing for you to be concerned about. You're too young to worry about such things. Now eat up".

I quietly ate my tea. Maybe I'd ask dad another time. After tea, dad went to change his clothes. It was almost half past six and beginning to get dark outside.

"I'm off to the West End bar with Arthur now. I hope he and Jeannie haven't had another row. She really nags him at times doesn't she? Not like you". Dad smiled at mum.

"Yes I know Jeannie can be a bit of a nag at times, but I think she takes on too much sewing. She's got three dresses to make and a pair of curtains. I told her that she's running herself into the ground. She needs to tell folk "no" at times. That and their Mary and her growing up problems. You can't really blame her, can you? And Arthur doesn't help. He doesn't get involved does he?" mum smiled back.

"Oh well", Dad replied, "not everyone is as happy as we are eh?" he winked at me.
I was happy. I had a new book to read that mum got from the library and I was content after eating my tea. I nodded in reply and went into the living room. Dad left. Mum cleared the plates away and came into the room.

"Do you want anything to drink? Speak now or forever hold your peace! When I come through, I'm not getting up again until I've finished reading my magazine, so if you want anything either you tell me now or you'll have to get it yourself".

I didn't want a drink, so mum went and finished up in the kitchen. I could hear her stirring the pan of broth. We always had broth on a Sunday followed by a roast chicken and then trifle for afters. My granny came round every Sunday and stayed until after teatime. Dad called her "The little woman" because she was tiny. But she always brought sweets for me and a packet of biscuits for mum and dad. She would ask what I'd learned at Sunday school and ask what the minister had preached. She didn't like how mum and dad never went to church. Mum said that the dinner wouldn't make itself and dad wasn't religious. Granny went to a church near to her house.

She lived two bus rides away but dad said that even with the limited buses on a Sunday, she wouldn't miss a meal at ours. Mum hit his arm when he said that. She laughed and told him to be quiet.

When mum had finished, she came and sat down in the living room.

I was already reading my book and mum had her magazine. After a while, mum stopped reading.

"I might be mistaken, but I can smell paint. Can you?" she sniffed.

I could. "It's Alex. He's painting the living room. Mrs. Strachan went with him and they got the paint. He said he'd be there until he finished the painting". I told her.

With that, there was a knock at our door. "Who's that?" mum asked.

"Dunno, I'll go and see". I ran to the door. It was Alex. "We were just talking about you. Mum smelled the paint. Do you want to come in?"

Alex shook his head. "No I came by to say

sorry about the smell. I've said sorry to your neighbour. I've left a window open but it really stinks up there".

"Who are you talking to?" mum came to the door. Alex introduced himself and again apologised for the smell. Mum nodded.

"I can remember when we painted in here. It lingered for ages. Are you off home now? Do you live far from here?"

Alex told us that he lived in Merchant street, two bus rides away, but he was going to stay the night with his aunt Irene in James street. He told us that his mum and dad were pleased to be moving in upstairs. The house they lived in hadn't a bathroom and only an outside toilet.

"So you have to go outside to go to the toilet? Where do you have a bath? Don't you get washed?" I wanted to know. I'd never seen an outside toilet nor a house without a bathroom. Mum nudged me. "Don't be so rude".

Alex looked at the ground. His face red. "Yes we go outside and down a path. The toilet isn't great. There's usually big spiders in there. We get washed by the sink in the kitchen. I've only had a bath twice in my life. Our house has been condemned and the council said we had the flat upstairs. I saw that the tenement was built in 1950. It's on a stone above the front door so it's only twelve years old then".

I shuddered at the thought of spiders. I hated them. And I knew I wouldn't like to get washed by the kitchen sink. Then I remembered the cats and James Street.

"I know James Street. I go past there on my way to school. There's a lady who has cats. Three fluffy cats. I always stroke them. The lady always says hello to me". I told mum.

"You'd talk to anyone". Mum replied.

"Oh that's my aunt. The cats are twinkle, fluffy and misty. They're Persian". Alex smiled. "Aunt Irene talks to anybody as well. Right, I have to go. See you tomorrow".

He left and we returned to the living room. Mum said he was nice. I agreed. We settled ourselves down and I started to read. There was a noise in the lobby. Then shouting. Mum looked at me.

"What's going on now? Honestly, you want a quiet night in and it sounds like a riot out there. Listen...is that Mr. Milne I hear? Oh no, Robbie must have opened the door and he'll have run out".

Mr. Milne always kept his door locked. If Robbie managed to get out, there was no telling where he would go or what he would do. Once, when he ran off, he managed to end up eight streets away. All the people in the tenement were out looking for him. Mr. Milne was beside himself with worry. He almost called the police, but Arthur found Robbie and brought him back. Now it seemed like Robbie was out again. Mum shook her head.

"That poor man has an awful job with the boy. I know he comes across as being quite nasty, but he really has a terrible time. Robbie will need extra looking after soon. None of us are getting any younger and Mr. Milne looks much older than he is. What a life he has!"

I nodded but I didn't fully understand. Our clock chimed. It was seven o'clock now. I listened to see if I could hear what was happening. A while later, about fifteen minutes, I heard Mr. Milne and Robbie going back upstairs. I knew it was them; Mr. Milne was talking and Robbie was singing Humpty Dumpty again.

"Well at least he's found him. Now maybe I can read my magazine". Mum looked at me. "Before I do, would you like some lemonade?"
I nodded. I was getting bored with reading the same page over and over. Each time I tried to read, there was a noise and it stopped me turning over. Mum said it was because I was too nosey. I had to know what was going on.
Mum came back through with a glass of lemonade for me and a cup of tea for herself. We made ourselves comfortable on the sofa and started to read. There was a knock at the door and a voice called out

"Yoohoo, it's only me. I've a favour to ask", it was Jeannie.

"Come through, we're just in the living room", mum called back.
Jeannie walked in with Jean behind her.

"Could you watch our Jean for me please? I'm so mad I can hardly speak. I told our Mary to be back at seven, you know how dark it gets now, and she argued the point with me. Said she's big and older and didn't want to be treated like a baby. I said she shouldn't act like one then. She said that she was going to Anita's and what was the problem? Oh we had a big argument. She ended up saying she'd be back at seven after I said I'd not allow her to go on the school trip. Anyway, she's not back yet. I'm mad but I'm worried as well".

Mum got up, "Come on in to the kitchen. Jean can stay here. The girls can play Ludo or some other game if they want to. You know where Mary is, nothing's going to happen to her. Come on, she's just trying it on. Have a cup of tea and calm down.

I've just poured one for myself, I'll get you one. Don't worry. Remember what we were like at that age".

Jeannie nodded. "Yes, I gave my mum and dad many sleepless nights. I suppose Mary takes after me in a way. She's headstrong and knows it all. You're right. She's trying to see how far she can go. I'll give her such a telling off when I see her. The little madam!"

She turned to Jean. "Behave yourself. I'll have a quick cup and then go to Anita's Honestly, your sister will have me grey haired before my time".

Mum and Jeannie went into the kitchen. Jean looked at me. "Mary's in big trouble now. Serve her right. She's been horrible all day. Mum's really angry. I'm a bit scared. There's going to be a right row when mum gets Mary. I'll just go to my bed. I don't like it when they shout at each other. Dad'll be back and I bet mum shouts at him as well. He didn't fix the iron and she wanted to get the clothes done for church tomorrow".

I thought for a minute. "I bet your mum could borrow our iron. Maybe you could stay here tonight. We have a camp bed that dad can set up in my bedroom. That'd be great. We could tell each other ghost stories, have some sweets and have a pillow fight. I'll ask when your mum goes out. It'd be like having a holiday wouldn't it?"

Jean was pleased. We took out the Ludo and started to play. After a while, Jeannie and mum came back through.

"It's quarter to eight. I'm going to get her now. Oh I'm so mad. Thanks for the tea. I'll be back soon. Now remember our Jean. You behave".
Jean nodded and smiled. "I will mum".
With that, Jeannie left. Mum came and sat on the settee.

"Who's winning? You're not cheating are you?" she laughed.

"No mum we're not cheating. Jean's winning so far, but I'll catch up soon". I loved playing Ludo.
Five minutes later Jeanie came running through the front door.

"She's not there. Anita says she left about quarter past seven. She says that Mary was talking about showing me how grown up she was and that she might have gone round to Moira's. I'm going there now".

Mum stood up. "Well this has turned out to be quite an evening hasn't it? I bet she's at Moira's place. Okay, you go and get her. Jean is okay here".

Jeannie left scowling and muttering. She was angrier than ever.

"I'd hate to be in Marys' shoes". I said to Jean. "She's really gone and done it now!"

Jean nodded. No one could tell what Mary would do. She was so stubborn. We played some more. Mum was happy to read the rest of her magazine. As the game finished, we heard the front door open again. It was Jeannie. She was in a real rage. Her face was red.

"She's not been there. Moira says that she hasn't seen our Mary since Friday after school when they walked home with Anita. But get this. Apparently Mary was telling them about the dance at Nevis Hall and she said she was going to try and go because there's a boy going that she likes. I asked who he was and Moira said that he was in a class two years ahead of them. Mary has been talking to him and he's put the idea into her head. I'm just going to the hall now. If she's there, she's going to be in big trouble".

Jeannie was livid. It was the type of thing I could imagine Mary doing. I'd seen her talking to the boy, John Greig, at break time at school. All the girls liked him. He smoked cigarettes and used swear words though. I thought he was a bit odd.

Mary often stood beside him in the queue at

dinner time. I wasn't surprised that she might have gone to the dance. Jeannie ran out.

Mum looked at us. "I wouldn't like to be in Marys' shoes tonight. Jeannie is so mad. It's the angriest I've ever seen her. Good job you two are behaving yourselves".

We kept quiet. I was thinking of all the times I wanted to go to the shops without telling mum. Granny gave me one shilling once, not so long ago, and I really wanted to go and spend it. Mum said I wasn't allowed to go as I'd buy rubbish. I put the money into my pocket and said I was going out to play, but I was really going to go to the shop. When I went downstairs, I got as far as the end of the street and I got scared. Mum would kill me if she found out, and I'd be kept inside for ages. So I never went. One part of me admired Mary though. She'd actually gone to a dance. By herself. Without telling her mum. Wow! I just wouldn't have the nerve to do that.

Jean must have thought the same thing. She looked at my mum and shook her head. "Mum said we always had to tell her where we were going. She says there's strange people out there and you never know what could happen. She says that we always have to be careful".
Mum nodded. "Yes, you never know who's out there. I always tell madam here to let me know where she's going and with whom".

"Typical Mary", Jean told my mum, "she's always doing things to upset mum. If she doesn't get her way, she stamps her foot and throws a tantrum. She slams doors as well. Last week mum said   she couldn't buy our Mary a magazine that she wanted, you know the one with the film stars in it, and Mary started shouting and crying. She was in a real temper with mum. She said that she hated mum and dad and she really hated me. She said that she wanted to run away and be a film star. That would show us all. Mum told her not to be so daft. Who would pay to see her? Mary locked herself in the bathroom. She didn't come out for ages".

Mum sighed. I think she wanted to laugh but she was trying not to. Jean continued.

"I've seen the magazines with film stars in them. They all sit like this", she sat on the chair and crossed one leg over the other and put her hand under her chin. "I think I'd look better like this though". Jean sat back in the chair and tilted her head to the left. "What do you think?"

Mum was really trying not to laugh. I looked at Jean. "Do you want to be a film star then?"

"No I'd rather be a pirate. I'd go on adventures and find treasure and sail a huge ship". Jean told us.

"Well I have to say, that's certainly different from being a star". Mum laughed.

"What do you want to be when you grow up?" Jean asked me.

I told her I wasn't sure. Some days I thought I'd like to be a ballerina. Other days I'd like to be an ice skater. Then again, other days I wanted to be an explorer and find the treasure at the end of the world. Mum said there was plenty of time for both of us to decide what we wanted to do. We had lots of years ahead of us and we should take our time and not rush to grow up. She said we should enjoy our childhood because when we did grow up, we'd miss being able to play and run around without any cares. Jean and I listened quietly. We loved playing out on the green. We didn't have any cares other than what games we should play, what time our food would be on the table and what time we had to be inside.

Our life was a whole round of school, playtime, eating and bedtime. Summer holidays stretched out forever it seemed. Christmas and birthdays were exciting. Our parents were always there and we enjoyed life. We didn't know how much until our lives were turned upside down so horribly and so disastrously that weekend.

CHAPTER 4

Jeannie returned. It was just after half past eight. She was beside herself with anger clenching her fists and biting her bottom lip. I'd known Jeannie and Arthur Mclintock for all my life. They lived next door to us and they were my mum and dads best friends. I had seen Jeannie angry before; once when Mrs. Robertson accused her of taking a pillowcase from the washing line. It wasn't Jeannie, it was someone from the other tenement. And the second time was when she heard someone saying that Mary was a spoilt little brat and needed a good hiding. But now Jeannie was so angry that she could hardly speak. Mum was worried. She made Jeannie sit down and tried to calm her by asking her to tell her what had happened.

"I got to Nevis Hall and it was packed. I started asking the kids if they knew Mary. Some of them did. I asked if they had seen her and none of them had. Then I asked the woman at the door if she knew Mary. She said she thought she'd seen a girl like her go into the hall but she left about half an hour before I got there. She was with a boy. I asked who he was. No one seems to know. I don't know what to do. Do you think I should go and get Arthur? What if she comes home and I'm not there? I don't know anymore. I'm worried sick". Jeannie burst into tears.

I'd never seen Jeannie cry before and Jean

was upset as well. Mary certainly knew how to panic people.

"Well if I were you, I'd go and get Arthur. Do you want me to get him while you stay here? If Mary comes back, you should be here. Just in case". Mum always knew what to do.

"Would you?" Jeannie asked between sobs. "What if something's happened to her? Where could she be? Why is she doing this? I could kill her but I just want her home and safe".

Jean was sobbing by now. I wasn't sure what to do or say to help so I asked if she wanted another glass of lemonade. She nodded. But before I could go and get it, Jeannie spoke.

"I can't sit here and wait. I need to go and look for our Mary. Your mum won't be too long. Girls listen, I'm going downstairs to see if Mrs. Bruce has seen her. Will you two be okay by yourselves for a short time?"

Jean and I said we would be fine, so Jeannie left. I'd never been in the house by myself before. Okay, Jean was there as well, but I meant without one of my parents. It was exciting but odd.

"I don't want to go home". Jean started to cry. "Please ask your mum if I can stay. There's going to be such a row tonight. I don't want to be there".

I hugged her. I gave her some lemonade and told her I would ask. After all, she was my best friend. I would help her if I could. We sat by the fireside. It was warm and the flames leapt like ballerinas dancing on stage. We didn't talk. I wondered where Mary was and what was going to happen. Mary had gone somewhere with a boy. A boy! Oh she was in such trouble. Where on earth could she have gone to though? The only other place nearby where people went was the gardens. A piece of land was kept pretty by the local council. Lots of roses were planted and there were a few benches to sit on. Sometimes we'd go for a Sunday afternoon walk in the summertime and we'd end up sitting by the gardens. Dad loved the peace and quiet. I liked to play on the grass verges. I would pretend I was on an island and there were sharks on the gravel paths between the rose beds. Mum often made egg sandwiches and took a flask of tea with her. We loved having a picnic there. Mum once said that couples who were in love often went and sat there at night. I told Jean.

"Do you think Mary and the boy have gone there? Should we tell your mum?" I asked Jean.

"I bet that's where she is. Yes we'll tell mum when she comes back". Jean had cheered up a bit.

"Mum'll need to take a torch with her. There's no lights near to the gardens. Oh I wonder if Mary is kissing the boy."

We giggled at the thought. As we were imagining it, Jeannie returned.

"Why are you two laughing? This is serious, Mary's missing and all you two can do is sit here and laugh? Have you no feelings at all? I'm ashamed of both of you. Jean you should know better. This is your sister that we're upset about". Jeannie was angry. She grabbed Jean by the shoulders and shook her.

"Mum! Mum stop it!" Jean shouted back at her mum. "I didn't do anything. Honestly. Stop it mum!"

My mum came into the living room followed by dad and Arthur Mclintock.

"What are you doing? Leave her alone. She's not doing anything!" Arthur shouted at Jeannie.

Jeannie stopped shaking Jean. She sat down on the settee and started to sob. Arthur sat next to her.

"Don't worry. We'll find our Mary. She'll be in one of her pal's houses. Knowing her, she'll come home as if nothing's happened. I bet she turns up anytime now".

Jeannie nodded her head. "It's just that she's never done anything like this before. If I only knew where she was. I'm worried sick. I know she can look after herself, but there's all sorts out there and you just never know..."

Jeannie started to cry again. Arthur looked at dad.

"We could go and knock on doors and see if she's anywhere in the tenements. There's a chance that she's gone in somewhere to talk to someone and lost track of time. We could start upstairs and work our way down. Then go into the next block".

Dad agreed and off they both went. Mum sat next to Jeannie.

"I know it's not much help, but you two have been arguing all day and you know what girls of that age are like. She's just being a typical kid. It'll work out okay. Like Arthur said, she'll walk in as bold as brass and wonder what the fuss is about. Now come on, I'll put the kettle on while the men go and knock on the doors".

This seemed to cheer Jeannie up. She looked at Jean. "I'm sorry I shouted at you and shook you. It's just that I'm worried. I shouldn't have taken it out on you though".

Jean nodded. She was still upset, but I could see that she understood how her mum felt. "It's okay mum. I'll be good".

I thought Jeannie would cry again. She went into the kitchen with mum. "I think I should go next door. You never know. Mary might turn up and if she tries to get in, the doors not locked but I won't be there and she'll panic. Jean you come with me".

I heard mum reply that she thought it might be a good idea. I thought mum might go with her, but she didn't. Jeannie came through.

"Come on our Jean. It's your bedtime anyway. Your dad can sort out this mess. I've had enough. Mary has pushed me as far as she can. You come home with me now".
Jean didn't say anything. I knew that she didn't really want to go back to their flat, but she saw how upset her mum was, so she went with her. After they'd gone, mum came through to the living room and sat next to me on the settee.

"Well you can't say that it's not exciting round here. I expect there'll be hell to pay when Mary turns up. I wouldn't want to be in her shoes".

"Where do you think she is mum?" I wanted to know.

"Do you think she's gone to the gardens with a boy? Do you think Jeannie will slap her when she gets home?"

Mum looked at me. She was very serious. "I don't know where she is. I only know that she's caused a real upheaval. Poor Jeannie has had enough to deal with, what with all the sewing she does and then Mary always being cheeky and arguing with her. Now this. I feel sorry for her. Arthur needs to take Mary in hand. She ignores her mum, but I couldn't see her being cheeky to her dad. Arthur can be very strict when he's pushed".

We sat together looking at the fire. Mum had her arm round me and I felt safe. I was worried about what had happened to Mary, of course, but I was also worried about Jean. She was scared. She didn't like her parents to fight and she knew that Mary, once she came back, would cause big problems. I was thinking about this when dad came in.

Mum looked up at him. She was concerned. "Any word yet?"

He shook his head. "Only thing we've learned is that Mary left Anita's. Anita might know something but she's not saying what. I talked to Mr. Milne upstairs. He hadn't seen her. He said that Robbie had managed to open the door and run out before he knew. Apparently Robbie was in the back green when he managed to catch up with him. Mr. Milne didn't see hide nor hair of Mary. He said he wasn't looking though. He was too busy trying to get Robbie. Robbie came to the door but all he said was 'Mary. Shed' Mr. Milne told me about what had gone on this afternoon between Mary and Robbie down by the drying shed. I've knocked at Mrs. Robertson's but no one was in".

"No there won't be. Mrs. Robertson goes to bingo every Saturday night. She won't be back until after ten. I don't know about Bunty though". Mum told dad.

I sat up. "I do. Bunty and Brian were going out, he told me. They were going to the pictures. He had to be back, I think he said about quarter to eight".

"Well they wouldn't have seen her would they? Arthur's gone to the police. They can go round and ask people. There's only so much we can do". Dad sat down on the sofa. "So much for my quiet night eh?"

Mum went to make him a cup of tea. It was then that I remembered something. "Dad, Mary might have run away".

Dad sat up. "Why do you say that? Is there something you know?"

"Well, at school, one dinner time, Annie Simpson was telling us all that during the holidays her granny and granddad took her to Butlins. They had a great time. Her granddad won the knobbly knees competition and her granny won the best granny one. She said there was a beauty queen competition and that Mary would easily win it. She said there was money if you won. Mary said she would like to go and win and use the money to buy clothes and to be a film star". I looked at mum who had come into the room with dad's cup of tea. "Honestly, that's what she said".

Mum shook her head. "Well I wouldn't put it past Mary to do something like that. We should have a word with Jeannie and tell the police as well. Mary could be anywhere by now if she's run away".

Dad agreed. "She would have needed to take the bus to the station and catch a train. I'll tell Arthur when he gets back".

Mum said he should go and tell Jeannie. Dad went to their flat. In a few seconds Jeannie came running into our living room followed by Jean. She grabbed me by my shoulders.

"Tell me everything. Tell me about Butlins". She was crying.

Mum pulled her away. Jeannie was shaking and red faced. Mum wasn't pleased. She glowered at Jeannie.

"Jeannie Mclintock, we've known each other since we both moved into this tenement and that was many moons ago. I've seen you upset over lots of things and I know that you're really in a state now, but if you ever come into my house and treat my child like that again, I swear I will knock you into the middle of next week! Now sit down and listen to what she's telling you!"

Jeannie sat down. She looked at mum and then at me. "I'm sorry. I'm just so wound up about this whole situation. I won't do anything like that again".

I told her what I knew; what Annie Simpson had told us and what Mary had said. Jeannie shook her head.

"I wouldn't put it past our Mary to try and run away to be a beauty queen. Her heads full of film stars and being famous".

Mum said we had better tell the police when they came back with Arthur. Dad was standing in the hallway by our front door. He came in. "They're back".

Arthur walked in with a man behind him. He said he was a detective. He asked me questions about Mary and I told him about Butlins. He looked at Jeannie.

"We get this sort of thing all the time. Girls with their heads full of nonsense. We'll sort this out, don't you worry".

He turned to Arthur. "We'll just go and ask the local folk in the tenements if they've seen your daughter. Do you have a picture of her?"

Arthur nodded. "I'll go and get one. We've already been asking people if they're seen Mary. We asked in this block and the one next door to it. No one's seen hide nor hair of her".

Jeannie, Arthur and Jean left. Dad looked at me.

"It's time you were in bed. It's been quite a night. I expect the police will find the little madam".

I didn't want to go to bed just yet. I really wanted to know what had happened to Mary. I wasn't sleepy and I told dad. He said I should get my pyjamas on anyway. Mum went into the kitchen to get me a cup of warm milk. There was a knock at our door. It was Arthur.

"They're getting a policewoman to stay with us. Jeannie's in a right state. She can't stop crying. They're putting a generator with lights in the back green. They want all the keys to the coal sheds".

"Why?" mum asked.

"Well maybe she's managed to get locked in one". Arthur told us.

"I can't see that happening", mum shook her head, "how on earth would it? Mind you, saying that, I remember when Peter Bruce got locked in his granny's shed. It was open and a gust of wind blew the door shut. It pushed him over and he landed on the coal. He was only found when Mrs. Robertson went to hang out the clothes. He'd been in there for half an hour. Mrs. Bruce thought he was playing".

Dad nodded. He said that it was possible and he went with Arthur to open our shed. I asked mum why he went. She said it was to give Arthur support. That the Mclintocks' were beside themselves with worry. That Mary was stupid to have run away, that is if she had gone away. Mum still thought that Mary was hiding somewhere because she'd hidden once before. Jeannie had given her into trouble because she had been cheeky at school. When Jeannie turned her back, Mary ran out of the flat. She was found in our flat under my bed. Mum had gone to get the washing in and left the door open. I was with her. Jeannie had been looking for Mary for about twenty minutes.

I had changed and was sitting in the living room with mum when Mrs. Robertson came to our door. She had seen the police and wanted to know if there was anything she could do to help. Mum thanked her and told her what was going on.

"That young girl needs a good talking to". Mrs. Robertson tutted as she left. I was glad she'd gone, but I had a feeling of dread and I couldn't say why. I would soon know.

CHAPTER 5

When I finished drinking my milk, I put the cup into the kitchen sink. I still didn't feel sleepy and, being nosey, I wanted to see what was happening in the back green, so I went into my parent's bedroom. I liked my parent's room. The walls had light pink wallpaper and the curtains were pink with a white floral pattern. Their top cover was pink and white. Mum said it was a candlewick bedspread. It felt nice and soft. The curtains were open and I saw the policemen put two huge lights on the green. They had a machine, that my dad later told me was a generator, and it turned on the lights. I saw two policemen opening and looking in the coal sheds. I knocked at the window to wave to dad, but he couldn't hear me. Mum came through.

"Why are they putting lights there? And why is dad standing by that light with Arthur?" I really wanted to know. "They couldn't see into the sheds without them. Dad's there to help Arthur". Mum stood beside me and looked out. A policeman went past dad and walked into the drying shed. I thought he was brave because of the ghost in there. I knew that I would never be able to go in. The thought of a ghost made me shake. It scared me. Then it all happened. He came running out and went to another policeman. They went into the shed together.

There was a shout. The man who was the detective ran down the green into the shed. I looked at mum. I didn't know what was happening.

"What's going on? Why are they all going into the shed?"

Mum didn't say anything. She just stood there quietly but I saw her eyes fill with tears. Then she put her hand up to her mouth and said

"Oh god no! Oh dear sweet Jesus no! It can't be. Oh god no!"

I was confused. Why was mum praying. And why was she crying? Then Arthur left dad and ran into the shed.

A policeman grabbed his shoulder before he could go inside, but he pushed him away and went in. I heard another shout. Dad ran after Arthur. Mum pulled my arm.

"Come away. Come on, this isn't something for you to see". Mum was still crying but she was trying to hide it from me.

I didn't move. There were more policemen who went into the shed. Then Arthur came out with dad. Dad had his arm round Arthur's shoulders. Half way up the green, Arthur fell onto his knees. He started shouting. Dad knelt beside him. I could hear what he was shouting even above the noise of the generator.

"Mary, my Mary", he kept shouting over and over again.

I looked at mum. I didn't understand what was going on. Arthur and dad kneeling on the green and mum crying. I knew I shouldn't keep asking, but I was really worried. I'd never seen anything like this before. Well, that was a lie. I suddenly remembered Jack Norris. He lived in the far tenement and dad said he drank a lot. I drank lots of water but dad said it wasn't water it was the 'demon drink'. Then one day, Jack went onto the green and started shouting that he had been saved.

We were all playing and we stopped to listen. It was very peculiar. He stood there in the middle of the green and waved a bible about. Mrs. Robertson came out and tried to move him away but he said that she needed saving as well. I don't know who it was, but someone got the police and Jack was taken away. Mum said he was taken to a hospital. I asked mum what Jack was going on about and she said that he's found Jesus. Dad said that he didn't know Jesus was missing. Mum hit him on the shoulder and said it wasn't the poor man's fault, and that drink had addled his brain.

So I had seen something similar to what was going on. But I couldn't understand why Arthur kept calling Mary's name. Mum pulled me away and closed the curtains. We went into the living room. She sat on the settee beside me and pulled me close.

"Mum, I can't breathe". She held me so tightly that it hurt.

"Sorry, I'm just a bit upset". She brushed her tears away.

We heard a noise in the lobby. Arthur had come upstairs and was making a sort of wailing sound. I wondered if dad was with him.

He was. Dad came into the living room. He

looked at mum and shook his head. That started mum off crying again. I asked dad what was going on.

"Nothing for you to be worried about. Now, come on, it's past your bedtime. You need your sleep. Through you go. We'll be in shortly".

I knew dad wanted to speak to mum, so I left. Dad shut the door. He never did that, so I reckoned it was serious. I sat in my bed and cuddled my teddy. Mum said I was getting too big to sleep with a teddy bear, but I loved it. Then I heard a noise. A loud scream followed by a door banging and people running down the stairs. I was curious so I crept into my mum and dads' bedroom again and looked out at the green. Jeannie was running towards the drying shed. She was screaming. Arthur followed her with a policeman. She ran into it. Dad came through.

"I thought I told you to go to bed. Now come on, go through". He was angry with me.

"I heard Jeannie screaming and I just came to see what was wrong". I started crying. "I'm scared".

Dad took me through to my bedroom. He hugged me. As we sat there, we heard noises from the lobby. Jeannie was sobbing hysterically and I heard Arthur speaking. Dad left me for a short while.

"I'll be back just now, I'm just going to see Arthur. You stay here, mum will be through shortly. Now promise me that you'll stay in bed this time".

I promised. I heard the front door open and

59

dad talking. I lay as still as I could, trying to hear what was said. I was curious but scared as well. He wasn't gone for long. Mum came into my room. She stood by the window and looked out at the street. The lamplight shone just outside my window. I saw mum had been crying again. I knew, I just knew it was about Mary.

"Mum where's Mary?" I knew it wasn't good to ask questions, but I needed to know.

Mum pulled my curtains and turned round. "Mary's gone". She didn't say anything else. I was confused. But knew it would be better if I asked dad.

Dad finally came into my room. He spoke very quietly.

"The police have sent for Father Fitzpatrick. He'll be here soon. They're checking a few things and they have things to do then they'll move you know what".

He turned to me. "I'm sorry but you won't be able to go and play on the back green for a while".

"Why not?" I had to know. "It's not fair. Just because Mary's missing. Has she really run away? Did she kiss a boy?"

Dad came and sat down on the bed. He was serious.

"Dad", I was curious, "mum says Mary has gone. Where has she gone to? Annie Simpson went with her granny to Butlins and said there was lots to do.

Mary said she wanted to go and if her mum didn't let her she'd run away. I told Jeannie that.

Has Mary gone to Butlins?"

Dad coughed. "No she's not there. She's gone to heaven to be with Jesus".

He sounded upset. I was confused. My granny and granddad died and went to heaven. So Mary was dead. But she was young. And wasn't it only old people who died and went to heaven? I asked dad.

"Don't ask so many questions. Mary's gone. Now, come on its past your bedtime. Lay down and try to sleep".

I looked over at mum. She had tears in her eyes.

"Do you want to leave on the bedside light?" she came over and kissed my head.

I shook my head. "No mum. It's okay". I turned over and hugged my teddy.

Mum closed my door. I could still hear the noises from the lobby. There were lots of footsteps and a door banging shut. Then I heard Arthurs' voice. I wasn't sure what was being said, but he was talking to someone, then a door banged shut again.

I tried to sleep. But I couldn't. The whole evening was horrible. My mind played it over and over again. So Mary was dead. I wondered what she would do in heaven. At Sunday school we were told that people who died and went to heaven became angels. Would Mary be an angel? Would she wear a long white dress? Would she have big feather wings? Did that mean she could fly around? I'd love to fly around. Would she sit on a cloud? Would she play a harp? I couldn't imagine Mary playing a harp. She was good at playing the recorder; she played it in the school choir. And she could sing really nicely. I wondered what songs the angels sang. Did they sing hymns like we did at church, or did they have other songs to sing in heaven? And would she look like she did when she lived next door?

The pictures of angels in the hall where we had Sunday school showed them with long blonde hair and blue eyes.

Mary had reddish hair and brown eyes. So did everyone who became an angel change? Did their hair and eyes change colour when they went to heaven?

Or did that happen when they died? I had never seen a dead person, so I wondered when they knew that they were angels? Did angels ever get hungry or thirsty? What did they eat and drink?

All of this ran through my mind until I couldn't think any longer and I drifted off to sleep. But before I did, I made a mental note to ask the teacher at Sunday school next day, all the questions I had thought about.

I woke up in the early hours of the morning. The street light was still shining. Everything was still. Silence. It took me a few minutes to remember what had happened. The light shone through a gap in my curtains and made a shadow on the wall. It looked like a man. I pulled the blankets over my head and lay as still as I could. I was scared. Was that the ghost from the shed?

Had it come for me as well? I couldn't breathe properly under the blankets as I was too hot. So I tried to pull them down to my ears and I lay as quietly as I could. My teddy was next to me and I buried my head in its back. What if Mary had been taken by the ghost? What if it decided that she needed another girl to play with? I started to cry. My sobbing got louder and louder.

"Mum!" I couldn't help it. I just wanted my mum. "Mum! Mum! Mum!"

The bedroom door opened and mum came in. She turned on the light next to my bed. I sat up, still crying.

"It's okay". she talked softly. "You just had a bad dream. Would you like a glass of water? It's still early, 3am". She hugged me.

I nodded. I was still sobbing but not as much as before. "Mum I'm scared. Did the ghost in the shed get Mary?"

Mum shook her head. "There's no such thing as ghosts. You have too much imagination. I'll get you some water. Now put the idea of a ghost out of your head".

Mum came back with my glass of water and stayed with me for a while.

I looked around my room. It was the same as ever. Nothing had changed, yet I knew that everything had changed and we'd never be the same again. I finally fell asleep again and dreamt of angels.

CHAPTER 6

When I woke up, the sun was shining through my curtains. I sat up and rubbed my eyes. Did I dream everything from last night? Was it real? I couldn't make up my mind, so I got out of bed and looked out of my window. Everything looked the same. There were two women standing across the road, talking. I recognised them from the other tenement. Maybe it was a bad dream after all.

I went into the kitchen. My mum was standing by the cooker. She was singing. That proved it. It must have been a dream. Mum was singing a show tune. She always sang when she was working in the kitchen. It depended how she sang though. If she was happy, she sang loudly and it sounded good. If she was annoyed, she sang loudly but it was strained. Today she was singing her usual song,

'Que Sera Sera', but it was odd. It sounded sad. I sat at the table.

"Mum, did I dream about Mary last night? Is she okay?"

Mum turned and looked at me. "No you didn't dream it. Mary was taken to the angels yesterday".

It stopped me talking. It was real! I looked down. Mum had turned away again and wasn't singing any more. I felt like crying. I felt sad. Mum put the toast and coffee on the table.

"Come on, eat your toast and drink up your

coffee. We'll be late for church if you dawdle". Mum told me.

"Is dad coming to church as well?" I asked as I left the table.

"No why do you ask?" mum took my plate and put it in the sink.

"Well dad never comes to church does he? I just wondered if he would today, because of Mary?" I looked at mum. "Are Mr. and Mrs. Mclintock going to church? Will I see Jean?"

"I very much doubt it. After last night they'll want to be left alone. And don't you go bothering them. Jean won't want to come out.

Oh and remember what the policeman told your dad. No going out to play in the green, it's off limits". Mum went into the bedroom to get changed. "Dad's gone out to get the papers. He'll be back soon. Go and get changed". She shouted.

I wanted to go into mum's bedroom and look out of the window to see what was going on, but I would have to wait until she left the room.

I put on my pink dress; I hated it. It had a sticking out skirt and a white collar that made my neck scratch. Mum had left my white socks for me to wear by my bed. I was in the living room when dad returned.

"Dad, mum says that you're not going to church with us?" I asked him quietly.

"No I'm not. Why change the habits of a lifetime? Are you ready? Is mum getting ready?" Dad smiled at me. "Are you okay now, after your nightmare last night?"

I nodded. I felt a lot better, but I also felt sad. Mum came through.

"Well look at you, all dressed without a fuss. That's a first". Mum smiled.

Dad said that he would stay behind and cook the dinner for us. Mum said that was an excuse but she wasn't in the mood to argue. So we put on our coats, said goodbye and set off. When we got into the lobby, I wanted to knock on the Mclintocks door and ask how Jean was, but mum said I shouldn't. I couldn't hear any noise coming from their flat. Mum said they were probably in the living room. I asked how they would be feeling. Mum said she didn't know. She'd never gone through anything like a child's death and God willing she never would have to.

I decided that it was better if I didn't say anything else. I didn't want mum to cry again. Everything felt sad and odd. Usually there were noises in the tenement but today there was nothing. It was quiet.

We arrived at the church, there were people standing around talking. When they saw us, they stopped speaking. One of them, Mrs. Birnie, came over.

"Awful thing that's happened. Did you see her? Is it true that she was in a coal shed? Poor family. They must be so upset".

Mum took a deep breath. "I can't tell you anything because I was too busy looking after my daughter. I wouldn't say anything anyway because I respect the family".

Mrs. Birnie huffed and walked away. Mum

looked at me. "Some people just like to gossip. You'll soon learn who they are. If they don't know the truth, they make things up. You need to ignore those people".

I nodded. We went into the church. It was huge inside but had a musty smell. I loved looking at the stained glass windows and there were lovely flowers next to the choir. There were lots of people as usual. Mum nodded to some of them and we sat in our usual place. It was odd not having Mrs. Mclintock and Jean and Mary there. It felt like everyone was looking at us. It wasn't nice. I felt uncomfortable.

The service started. After we sang the first hymn, Father Fitzpatrick told the children to leave and go upstairs to Sunday school. I followed the teacher, Miss Kirkwood, and went into the upstairs hall. Chairs were set out in rows and in front of the rows stood a table with a collection box. Before we sat down, we had to put our money into the box. I often wondered why we did this. On this particular Sunday, whether it was because of Mary, I finally asked the question. Miss Kirkwood told us that the money went to Jesus.

"But how does Jesus get the money? How does it go up to heaven? Will Mary get some of it? And why does he need it? Are there shops in heaven where he can spend the money?"
Miss Kirkwood glared at me. Everyone else was silent. I waited for an answer but nothing was forthcoming. I asked again. Miss Kirkwood replied.

"It just goes to heaven. I don't know what he does with it. No one knows, it's not something we've ever asked. I don't know if Mary will get any. Now take your place and sit down".

I wasn't satisfied. "But why did Jesus want Mary to be in heaven? Did he want a friend? Will Mary have blonde hair and blue eyes now that she's an angel?"

Miss Kirkwood looked annoyed. Once again she replied that she didn't know anything as no one had ever seen an angel to ask one. That made me ask another question.

"If no one's ever seen an angel, how do you know what they look like?"

Miss Kirkwood now looked uncomfortable. She told me to be quiet and we should get on with our bible studies. Annie Simpson was sitting next to me. She whispered in my ear,

"You shouldn't ask these questions. It's not right. Did you see Mary? What did she look like? Was it awful?"

I whispered back to her that I hadn't seen anything because my mum and dad said I wasn't to keep looking out of the window and they pulled the curtains. Annie looked disappointed.

"I would have gone down and had a look", She said. "Even if my mum and dad said not to, I would have gone".

I shook my head. I didn't want to talk or think about it. All I knew was that Mary was dead. I felt upset again. I wanted to cry.

My face was hot and I felt tears pricking my eyes. The teacher saw me. She came over and talked to Annie.

"First of all, the people who live in the tenement are all very upset by what has happened. No one knows for sure how Mary died.

And now you're upsetting everyone by bringing the subject up. We're here to learn about the bible, Jesus and God. So let's all settle down and learn something". Miss Kirkwood was strict when she needed to be.

The rest of the Sunday school session dragged on. As it always did and it seemed like a lifetime. I didn't like being there. Truth be told, I only went because mum promised that I could have a bar of chocolate after I returned home. I always looked forward to Sundays, just because of the chocolate. Finally we finished and I ran downstairs to meet my mum. She stood by the entrance to the church. I told her what had happened and she wasn't pleased with me.

"When will you learn not to ask questions? And especially in Sunday school. Honestly, you're going to get into trouble one of these days!"

I didn't reply. There was nothing I could say that wouldn't cause a row, so I remained silent. As we began to walk toward home, a woman came over and talked to mum.

"Isn't it awful? That poor girl, murdered like that. I wouldn't be able to sleep if I lived in your tenement".

Mum was livid. She stood with her hands on her hips. "And how do you know that she was murdered? Were you there? Did you see it? No, I thought not. You're spreading rumours. Who told you these things?"

The woman blushed. "I..I heard".

Mum replied, "Well unhear. Its people that spread rumours who do most damage. How would you feel if that were your child? You wouldn't be happy would you? Please have some thought for the family. Thank you!"

I had never seen mum so angry. I hid behind her and watched. I thought the woman was about to faint. Her face turned red and she looked like she was about to cry. Mum took my hand and pulled me away. We walked home very quickly. So quickly, in fact, that I had to run to keep up with her. When we turned into our road, there were two policemen standing at the doorway of out tenement. They stopped us.

"What business do you have here missus?" one of them asked mum

As if she wasn't angry enough! I tried to make myself invisible by looking at the pavement. Mum was not happy.

"We live in flat three. Now if you don't mind, I'd like to go upstairs and have my dinner. Excuse me please".

The policeman stepped aside and apologised.

"Sorry missus, I didn't realise. My apologies". Mum said she knew he was doing his job but would it be like this every time we wanted to go out or in? He said it might be for a short while. Mum tutted and stomped up the stairs. We went inside and into the living room. She looked at dad.

"It's not right. Having to tell them who I am each time I go in or out. And when can we use the green? I have washing to do and it won't dry inside", she turned to me "and madam here is going to get fed up being inside. She'll drive me crazy. Honestly, this is awful".

Dad told her that it would take time for the police to sort things out. I went to my room and changed my clothes.

Mum went to hers to get changed. I sat on my bed and listened for mum leaving her bedroom then I crept in and looked out of the window. There were four policemen standing by the drying shed. There was tape all around it and over the entrance. For the first time that I could remember, there wasn't a soul on the green. It was odd. Even on a Sunday there were usually one or two children playing. I didn't like the silence either. Even Mr. Milne and Robbie were quiet. Everything had changed. I wondered what had happened to Mary. Was she killed? Or did she see the ghost and it scared her? Did she just suddenly fall down dead? If I fell down would I die?

I went back to my room and sat on the bed. If I fell off the bed, would I die and become an angel? I looked at my reflection in the small mirror on the dressing table. I had brown hair and blue eyes. I imagined myself as an angel with blond hair.

I lay on my bed and crossed my arms over my chest. I thought that was how an angel would look but I tried to feel like an angel would feel, good and happy. I was getting there when mum came in.

"What on earth are you doing? I need you to set the table. And why are you lying like that on your bed?"

I explained," I wanted to see what I'd be like as an angel".

Mum shook her head. "Whatever next will I get from you? Come on, set the table. Now!"

I decided that I would try to be an angel for the rest of the day. I went into the kitchen and set the table for dinner. After doing so, I stood back. Mum was stirring the broth. I smiled as angels do.

"What are you smiling about?" mum asked me. "Stop it. It's unnerving".

I decided to go into the living room where dad was reading the Sunday papers.

Maybe mum didn't appreciate me being an angel because I didn't have my hands clasped in front of me like I did when I prayed at church. So I stood by the door and smiled with my hands pressed together. It took a few minutes before dad noticed I was there.

"What's wrong?" He put the paper down. "Why are you standing like that?"

He called mum who came in and hit me on my shoulder. She told me to stop and that it was in bad taste. I said that I just wanted to see what it was like being an angel. Dad coughed and picked up the paper. He held it in front of his face. Mum told me that I would have to mend my ways. Then I might have a chance of eventually getting to heaven but if I kept on as I did then I might get there sooner than I expected. As I left the room I heard dad laugh.

I felt hungry. The smells coming from the kitchen made me want to eat immediately. Mum's wonderful broth, roast chicken and cabbage were my favourite Sunday dinner. I looked forward to it all week.

We ate at the same time every Sunday. 1.30pm. Granny always came to dinner. She lived a good half hour away, and dad said that she'd get to our flat quicker if she didn't stop to talk to everybody she met on the way. Granny talked a lot. Dad said that he could never get a word in edgeways. Mum said that granny knew all the gossip. Dad said that granny was a magnet for gossip. But I liked granny. She always brought me sweets. Sometimes she made toffee and she once made fudge, except it stuck to my teeth and I couldn't talk for a while. Mum said that granny should make it more often as it was the quietest she'd ever known me to be.

So we waited for granny to arrive. Mum told dad to watch at the living room window and give her a shout when he saw granny coming down the street. I was hungry and I hoped granny wouldn't be too long.

CHAPTER 7

Dad and I stood at the living room window and watched for granny. I had to stand on my tiptoes to see out. She finally came into view.

"Your mother's here". Dad shouted to mum, "and she hasn't got her broomstick. Oh but she does have a dead bird on her head".

I giggled. Mum came through. "Don't be horrible. She saved up for ages to buy that hat. It's her pride and joy".

Dad laughed. "She should have gone to the butchers when he plucks the chickens. She could have had lots of feathers for nothing".

"That hat cost a lot of money". Mum told me. "I'll just heat the broth up. You let granny in".

Dad winked at me. "A lot of money? Well she was robbed. They saw her coming. I wonder what doom and gloom she'll talk about today. No doubt it'll be about next door. Funny how awful things spread so quickly. Yet if there's good news, no one wants to know".

I went to the door and opened it. There wasn't a sound in the lobby. That was odd. Usually I would hear the Mclintocks or Robbie, but today it was silent. I was puzzled. After what seemed like ages, I heard granny huffing and puffing as she came up the stairs.

"Those stairs will be the death of me one day. I swear they get steeper each time I come round. I was just talking to Mrs. Bruce. Come on young lady, give your old granny a hug". She held her arms out.

I did. I loved granny. She was funny and easy going and always on my side if I got into trouble from mum and dad. I loved the smell of her lavender perfume. We went into the house. Granny gave me her coat and hat to put into my bedroom. I placed them on my bed.

She opened her handbag and gave me a bag of sweets. We went into the kitchen where mum was serving the dinner.

Mum took the sweets and put them into a cupboard.

"You can have them later. If you eat one now it'll spoil your dinner. Go and tell dad it's ready".

I couldn't see how one sweet would spoil a meal and I thought it was mean of mum to take my sweets away. I crossed my arms and sulked for a while.

Dad came through and we sat at the table. Mum served the broth. Dad always had the biggest plate. Mum said it was because he worked hard all week and deserved the most food.

"This is very good broth", granny nodded as she sat back in the wooden chair, "I taught you well. I remember my own mother teaching me to make it". She looked over at me, "Have you been watching your mother making this? It's about time you started to learn how to cook. When you get married your husband will expect you to make nice meals".

I pulled a face, "I'm never getting married. I'm going to be an ice skater and travel round the world. I'll wear a pink dress – one that hasn't a scratchy collar – and I'll twirl around".

Mum laughed, "And where round here are you going to skate? There aren't any ice rinks in this area as far as I know".

I didn't say anything. I was a bit annoyed. Granny noticed and replied, "Well she's young. Let her dream", she changed the subject, "awful about that girl next door, what's her name. That's just what happens nowadays. You never know what's ahead of you.

I was just saying to Irene Buchan last week, if I knew then what I know now, I'd have moved to the country years ago. Sometimes I don't feel safe in my own house".

Mum nodded. She kept eating her broth. Dad hadn't said anything but now he looked at granny,

"I never knew you were a lover of the countryside. Why didn't you move?"

Granny stopped eating. She sat back and looked at us all.

"Well when I was first married, Jim and I had the offer of going to the Mackie's estate and working there. Jim would have been gamekeeper and I was going to work in the big house. Of course the war put paid to that. It was a shame because there was such a nice cottage to rent as well. We never moved. It was a horrible time. The girl next door was killed, just like here. A bomb fell on her".

I was confused. Did a bomb fall on Mary? How did that happen? I was about to ask when granny started speaking again.

"Well it didn't just fall on her, it fell on the whole house. Killed, stone dead. She had lovely hair didn't she?"

Mum looked at granny and asked how would, she know that granny's neighbour had lovely hair. Granny said that she was talking about our neighbour and mum should concentrate more. Mum rolled her eyes. Then granny went on.

"I remember the last time I saw her. She had on a beautiful green dress. Lovely it was. It suited her to a T. I said, 'That suits you. It really brings out the colour in your eyes'". I always thought she had the nicest eyes I ever saw. Of course she took after her grandfather. This is a lovely plate of broth by the way, yes, her grandfather was a character. Worked at the docks. Do they know how the girl died yet?"

Mum gathered the plates and put them in the sink. She started to serve the main meal.

"No, I don't know more than you do at this stage. How do you know Marys' grandparents then?"

Granny sighed. "What makes you think I know them?"

Mum gave us all a plate of food. "Well you just told us that her grandfather worked at the docks".

Granny was confused. "Did I? I don't think so. I was telling you about my neighbour. The one who was bombed", she looked at me, "did you know that girl who died? The one across the lobby? I keep forgetting her name".

I nodded. "Yes I did. Her name was Mary".

"Did you play together? What was she like?" granny asked.

I didn't want to reply. I felt sad just thinking about Mary, but I thought it would be rude not to answer granny. But before I could, mum replied.

"I don't think we should be talking about this at the dinner table. Can we change the subject please?"

Granny huffed and ate the rest of her meal in silence. Dad didn't say anything, he just coughed occasionally. Finally granny spoke.

"Of course, Mary was my friends name. She died as well. Awful thing. She slipped in the bathroom and hit her head. And that was that. Dead as a dodo. She had a lovely funeral though. Big turnout. Good hymns as well. I expect that poor girl next door will have a big funeral. So sad. Very sad thing to happen, poor girl".

Mum sighed. "Please don't keep on about death. It isn't nice to keep talking about it. I'd like to have my meal in peace".

But granny wasn't going to let it go. "I saw Mrs. Bruce before I came up the stairs. Terrified she is. Of course it's different for her, what with her being a widow and all. And her living in the bottom flat. You never know who's out there. She was saying that she felt terrible. Can't say I blame her. This trifle is good but it could be doing with a bit of sherry in it. Now where was I? Oh yes, Mrs. Bruce. She's a nice woman. I've always liked her. She said she's keeping her door locked until the police sort things out".

Mum put her spoon down and looked sternly at granny. I knew she was annoyed.

"Look, I won't say it again. Will you please stop talking about what's happened. Thank you". Granny wasn't pleased. She told mum that she didn't mean anything bad, just that Mary was the topic of conversation on people's lips and she was just saying what everyone else said.

After dinner, and before she went into the living room, granny sneaked into mum and dads bedroom and looked out at the green. I joined her.

Two policemen stood by the drying shed. Two other policemen stood halfway up the green. Granny tutted. She said it was a dreadful business. I told her that Mary was horrible to all of us before she was missing. And I wondered why she had died. Granny said it happened sometimes. That there were odd people around and we had to be careful from now on until the police did their work. I wasn't sure what she meant, but it sounded serious.

We went into the living room and mum served us all a cup of tea. Mum told granny about what the women said before and after church. Granny sat back in her chair.

"Well the thing is, people gossip. And as you know, nothing really happens around here. The biggest thing was when that boy, you know the one I mean, stole the meat from the butchers shop.

Apart from that, there was nothing else that happened to speak of. Now whatever went on, and I'm not saying anything did, it's news for folk.

You live next to the family, you're friends with the mother and people just put two and two together. They make five. People talk. And it'll get worse before it gets better".

Granny must have been right because both mum and dad agreed with her.

After that, granny talked for a while about her friends.

It was almost four o'clock when granny decided to leave.

"I'm going to Rita Hendry's for my tea tonight. She's doing cold cuts and we're having ice cream afterwards. But I'm off to the cemetery just now. I'll just go home and get the flowers for Jims' grave then I'll go for my tea. I expect the young girl will have a good lot of flowers at her funeral. Is there any word about it yet? Won't be for a while I suppose. So sad. Poor girl". Granny told us all.

With that, granny got up then she turned to me.

"Can you fetch my coat and hat? There's a good girl".

I went to my room. Granny's hat lay there on top of her coat on my bed. I couldn't resist it. I tried on the hat. Looking in the mirror, I thought it was very pretty and suited me. Blue and green feathers covered it. I thought that it should belong to a mermaid. I imagined myself sitting on a rock by the seashore, with a long green tail, seashell beads and wearing the hat. As I was admiring myself, mum came in.

"Are you sleeping? Granny's waiting to go. We thought you'd gone to bed. And take her hat off. She'll not be pleased if you mess up the feathers. Come on and say goodbye".
I did as I was told. Before granny left she looked at mum.

"Have you gone next door yet to see how they are? I would think with you being so friendly and all, they'd be pleased to see a friend.
Heaven knows, they're going to need all the friends they can get for the next few weeks if not months. If I was you, and I'm not telling you what you should or shouldn't do, heaven forbid, but I'd go and see them".

Mum thought for a minute. "Well I don't like to disturb them. And I don't really know what to say. It's difficult".

Granny nodded. "Yes it can be difficult but I'm sure you'll be okay".

Mum said she would think about it. Granny said she shouldn't think for too long. That the longer mum left it, the harder it would be. Then granny hugged me and left.

Dad helped mum wash and dry the dishes and I sat in the living room with my book. When mum came back through, she brought my sweets. I had forgotten about them. My mind was full of mermaids and hats. It had been a good afternoon. Mum smiled at me.

"I think your granny was right. I should go and see Jeannie".

CHAPTER 8

Mum made our tea. Cold chicken sandwiches cut into triangles. I wasn't very hungry as I'd eaten my sweets and I had a sore tummy. Mum wasn't happy with me. She tutted.

"I told you before not to be so greedy. Greed causes grief. Now look at you! You don't have to eat them all at once. I keep telling you this but you never listen. Well this is what you get!"
I knew she was right. I sulked for a while. I scowled and huffed and puffed to show how annoyed I was. Dad said that he agreed with mum. That made my tummy ache feel worse. Then after all our tea things were cleared away, mum brought up the subject of visiting the McLintocks.

"Do you think I should go and see how they are?" She asked dad. "After all, we are friends. It wouldn't do any harm would it? I mean, I'll just knock and ask if there's anything we can do, or if there's anything they need. You never know, they might need milk or bread or something. What do you think?"

Dad was reading the Sunday paper. He had his brown reading glasses on. He put it down and removed his glasses. "Well it's up to you. But just be aware that you might get the door shut in your face. People do odd things when they're grieving. The policewoman will probably answer the door though".

Mum said she'd forgotten about a

policewoman being there. I wanted to know if Jean was okay. I asked mum if I could go with her.

"I think it would be best if you stayed here. They'll not feel up to having visitors. We don't actually know what's happening at the moment, and we don't know how they're coping. Just leave it for now. I'll tell Jean that you were asking for her".

I felt a bit sad. I really wanted to see Jean and make sure she was okay. We usually played together all weekend.

Dad wasn't sure that mum was going to do the right thing, but he said that once she made up her mind, he couldn't stop her. So, a few minutes after we talked, mum went over to the Mclintocks door. She left our door open a little. I asked her why, and she said "just in case". I wondered what she meant, but didn't dare to ask. Mum told me to stay in the living room with dad, but I told dad I was going to the bathroom and I hid behind the front door and listened.

Mum knocked softly at first. She waited. There was no reply. She knocked a bit louder and waited. Just as she turned round, the door opened. A woman stood there. I'd never seen her before.

"Erm I live across the way and just wondered if there was anything that Jeannie and the family needed. You know, shopping".

The woman smiled at mum. "I'm W.P.C. Simpson. I'll be here for the duration. If the family need anything I'll let them know at the station and someone will get the items. Thank you for offering though".

I could tell by her actions that mum didn't know what to do or say. She looked across and saw me.

"I told you to stay inside", she turned to the policewoman, "Sorry about that. Can you let the family know that I was here and that we're thinking of them. Is there any word as to what happened to Mary?"

The policewoman said she'd tell the family that mum had offered help and no, there wasn't any news about the young girl. She shut the door. Mum came back into our flat. She went to dad. He sighed

"Did you see Jeannie at all?"

Mum shook her head, "That was really awkward. A policewoman answered the door.

Apart from her talking, I didn't hear a peep from the flat. It was almost like they weren't there. I wonder what's going on.

I asked if there was any news and the policewoman said no. So I suppose we'll just have to wait and see".

Dad agreed. I think he was secretly relieved. He went back to reading the papers. Mum got her magazine and sat by dad. I lay on the floor and played with my dolls house. It was made from old boxes that dad glued together and the furniture was made from match boxes. Jean and I often played with it when it was too wet to go outside. I missed her. I thought about Mary. Last time I saw her she was nice and waved to me.

Now I would never see her again. I started to think about her clothes. Would Jean still have to wear Marys' old clothes? Or would Jeannie put them in a box and keep them under her bed? What about Marys' hair ribbons? She had one that I really liked. Pink velvet. I thought it was the most beautiful ribbon I'd ever seen. Once, when I went to play in their flat, Jean let me see a bag full of different ribbons that Mary wore in her hair. I asked if Jean ever got to wear any and she shrugged and said she didn't like them much. Mary came into the bedroom. We thought she'd be mad, but she seemed pleased that I liked the ribbons. She even showed me the new dress that Jeanie had made her. It was pink and white and had a pink bow at the waist. That was almost a year ago. When Mary was nice. I wondered if Jean would get the dress. It would be an awful shame if she didn't. I wanted to ask mum but I was worried she might get upset. So I kept playing.

We were there in the living room when we heard a knock at the front door.

"Well that's strange." Mum said, "I wonder who that can be?" She went to answer it. We heard voices then mum walked in with Arthur behind her.

"Sorry to bother you but is there any chance that you might be able to give us some milk? The bottle we have seems to be off and Jeannie will only drink tea just now". Arthur looked tired.

His eyes were red and had black shadows

underneath them. He hunched his shoulders.

"How are you? How is Jeannie? Are you coping?" Dad asked him.

I had never seen a grown man cry before. Arthur suddenly burst into tears and sat on the settee crying loudly. I was scared. I ran to mum and put my arms round her. She started crying as well. Dad spoke quietly,

"Would you like a small glass of brandy? I'll get you one. We have half a bottle from Christmas. A few capfuls were put into the cake. Now come on, I'll not take no for an answer". Dad went to the kitchen and came back with a small glass of an amber coloured drink. He handed it to Arthur who drank it quickly.

"I'm sorry, it's just been awful. Jeannie cries all the time and poor Jean just sits there. We have a young policewoman staying with us during the day and a policeman at night. They've been terrific but it's the not knowing what happened to our Mary that's taking its toll. Did someone do something to her or did she have an accident? We just don't know. It's the waiting to find out that's the worst thing".

I felt sad. I tried not to cry but I was a bit scared. Arthur was a big man with red hair and he always had a smile on his face. The Arthur who was sitting in front of me was a different person. For some reason, I thought he appeared smaller and older. It wasn't nice. Mum went to the kitchen and came back with a jug of milk.

"Do you need anything else? What have you eaten today?"

Arthur looked sad. "We had some mince and potatoes. Jeannie didn't eat much. May be a mouthful. Poor Jean ate some but she's spending a lot of time just reading in the living room She sleeps on the settee. She says that she doesn't want to sleep in the bedroom because it reminds her of Mary. Poor girl.

She says she feels lonely in there now". Arthur burst into tears. He looked at dad. "Why? Why us? What have we done to deserve this? We've always been good to people, helped where we can. I've never harmed anyone and Jeannie would give people the clothes from her back.

We've always gone to church. We keep ourselves to ourselves. So, can you tell me Why has this happened to us?" Arthur sobbed.
Dad said that he didn't know why. That God works in mysterious ways. Arthur replied that if this was Gods' work then he didn't want to know God anymore. Mum was standing by the window. She had tears in her eyes as she listened to Arthur.

"Mum, can Jean come over for a while? Please mum. Please". I really wanted to see her.
Mum looked at Arthur. He had stopped crying and he nodded his head.

"It might do her some good to get out of the flat. She likes the policewoman and talks to her, but I can see that she wants to get away from Jeannie's constant crying. I'll see what Jeannie says though. Since all of this trouble, she won't let our Jean out of her sight. I said to her that

Jean needs other company but I'm worried about Jeannie. The doctor gave her a sedative to make her sleep. She slept for three hours but then she went into the living room and just sat there watching Jean sleep. She hasn't really talked about Mary yet".

Mum said she could go with him and see how Jeannie was and if Jean wanted to come back to ours, but Arthur said that it might be best if he talked to them.

There was a knock at the front door and mum went to answer it. She came back followed by Mrs. Bruce.

When Mrs. Bruce saw Arthur, she stopped talking to mum. She went over to the settee and sat beside him.

"Oh, poor man. I have no idea what you're going through and in truth I wouldn't want to know. It's bad enough when any adult dies, goodness knows it was awful when my Peter died. I cried for weeks if not months. It's such a loss, although I'm used to it now, but still, it's a loss. But a child! Awful business! You expect to go before your child. It's not natural for them to go first is it? I was just saying to Agnes Robertson that your Mary was such a beautiful girl. So young. It's tragic. To be taken so early in life, it's just so sad. Do you know what happened yet?"

I was quiet. I knew I shouldn't talk. But I remembered how she rowed with Mary the previous afternoon. It didn't seem right that she felt sad now that Mary had died.

Arthur shook his head. "We'll know more tomorrow. I need to get back now".

"Well let your good wife know that I'm thinking about her". Mrs. Bruce looked suitably sad. She kept dabbing at her eyes with a handkerchief.

Arthur said that he would and dad walked to the door with him. I sat on the rug in front of the fire. Mum asked Mrs. Bruce if she would like a cup of tea. Mrs. Bruce said not unless mum was making one because she didn't want to put mum to any trouble. Mum said it was no trouble and she went to boil the kettle.

Mrs. Bruce looked at me as I stood by the window.

"And what have you been doing today? My grandsons were going to come over but I told them not to. It's a shame that you're not allowed, on the green. Still, I expect it's for the best".

I sat down on the rug. "Mum says she hopes everything gets sorted out soon. She's got clothes to wash and she wants to hang them out while the weather isn't too bad".

Mrs. Bruce nodded, "I was just thinking the same. Awful business this. It affects us all not just the McLintocks'. Still, I suppose we'll know what happened one way or another soon enough".

Mum came in with two cups of tea and some biscuits. Dad followed her.

"Arthur's going to see if Jean can come over for a while. Now if she does," dad looked at me, "I want you to be good. She'll be upset and she might cry. If she does, just let her get it out of her system. This has been terrible for all of us but especially for the family. Remember they've lost a daughter and Jean's lost a sister. No matter how much they argued and carried on, Mary was still her sister".

I told dad that I'd be good. Mum and Mrs. Bruce started talking about Mary and what could have happened to her. Dad sat and rolled his eyes.

"You two are just gossiping. No one can tell what went on. The police will let us know all in good time, but if I were you, I'd keep my opinions quiet. You never know who might hear. If you say something and it's repeated, it could get back to Arthur and Jeannie and it might make matters worse".

Mrs. Bruce looked annoyed. She furrowed her brow. She drank her tea and left soon afterwards. Mum wasn't pleased with dad.

"What did you say that for? Now she'll go and tell folk that you were horrid to her. You know what she's like".

Dad sighed. "Yes I do know what she's like. But you can't gossip like that. She's the type of woman who'll take what you say and twist it. Best not to say anything at all".

Mum thought for a minute. "I suppose you're right. It's just that we don't know what's going on and it's worrying. Was Arthur okay when he left? You were talking for a while".

"He was saying that the policeman who's staying there at night told him that we're all going to be interviewed. I said that we had already spoken to that detective. Arthur said that Jeannie was still crying. She had an argument with Mary and she blames herself".

Mum nodded. "Yes Jeannie told me when she came here asking if I'd keep an eye on Jean. Poor Jeannie. Mary was a handful right enough".

We sat in silence after that. I kept thinking how it must feel to have someone die so suddenly. My thoughts were interrupted by someone knocking at the door. Mum answered. I couldn't quite hear what she was saying. I would have crept closer but dad was watching. When mum came back, she talked to dad.

"That was the policewoman who's at the McLintocks. She says that Arthur asked Jean if she wanted to come over for a while but Jeannie became hysterical and said that Jean had to stay with her. They've called the doctor again. Here's hoping he gives her a stronger sedative this time".

I was disappointed. I'd looked forward to seeing Jean again. Oh well, I thought, maybe I'd see her at school the next day. I hoped that Jean and her mum and dad were okay.

CHAPTER 9

It was almost eight o'clock when mum ran a bath for me. Every Sunday night I had to have a bath so I was ready for school next morning. I loved splashing around and pretending to swim. While I washed myself – well played really -- mum ironed my school uniform. I hated it. A grey Pinafore dress, white blouse, navy and grey tie and a cardigan. It was different from my last school uniform which was grey and red. I had started at the big school in September. It was called "The Academy". My pinafore wasn't bought at the shop where Bunty worked; mum said it was too expensive. Dad said we'd manage but mum asked Jeannie to make it for me. Jeannie made a lot of clothes. She was very clever with her sewing machine, mum said, even though it was a second hand one. When I finished washing, I put on my pyjamas and went into the kitchen. Mum had finished ironing and gave me a cup of milk and a biscuit. I was sitting at the table, happily watching mum cleaning my shoes when I heard shouting in the lobby.

"What on earth is going on out there?" mum put my shoe down and went to the front door. I wanted to see what the noise was so I followed her. We stood behind the door and listened. It was Jeannie's voice. She was shouting at someone. Dad had also heard the noise and he came and stood next to us. He wore aftershave and it was a bit strong, but I liked the smell.

"Do you think we should see what's wrong?" mum asked him.

Dad shook his head. "It's none of our business. Just leave it alone. Whatever is going on, I'm sure Arthur can sort it out".

We were behind the door for a little while longer, trying to figure out what was being said.

After a few minutes we were about to give up when someone started turning the door handle. It made me jump. I didn't expect anyone to try and come into our flat. Dad was annoyed and he opened the door.

"What on earth?" he said, but Jeannie pushed past him and stood in front of mum. She was crying and red faced, but I could see she was angry. Very angry.

"It's your fault!! She's dead because of you!! I hate you! You and your smug family and perfect life! My Mary's dead because of you!"

Jeannie was screaming and she leapt at mum. Luckily Arthur and the policewoman grabbed her. Jeannie sobbed hysterically. Mum was shocked. She didn't know what to say. Her face was white and her eyes were open wide. I was terrified and I started to shake. Dad was fuming. He clenched his fists and his lips were tight. He spoke quietly but firmly to Arthur.

"I don't know what's going on but there's no reason why your wife should blame my wife for Marys' death. Please take her inside".

Arthur looked at dad. He shook his head. "It was your wife who made my wife stay and have a cup of tea".

Before he could say anything else, Jeannie started to shout again

"You said she'd be okay. That she was at Anita's' and she would be fine. You said it would be okay to have a cup of tea. If you hadn't made that tea, I would have gone to get her and she'd still be alive. It's all your fault. You killed my little girl".

Mum stood there, stricken. She tried to speak but she couldn't. Tears were running down her face. Dad was livid. He put his arm round mum and tried to pull her away. I stood by mum. I wanted to go back into the living room but my legs didn't seem to work. It was scary seeing Jeannie so upset, but it was also fascinating.

I had never seen anyone having hysterics before and I couldn't bring myself to stop looking at her.

Jeannie started pulling at her hair. Normally it was tied back in a bun, but now it was loose around her shoulders and it didn't look like she had combed or brushed her hair since Saturday morning. She kept tugging it and then she started to hit the wall next to our door with her open hands. Arthur tried to pull her away but she pushed him and hit him as well.

Then she turned to me. "You hated our Mary. Why? You're as nasty as the rest of them. Are you happy now? She's gone! I'll bet it pleases you doesn't it?"

By now Jean had come to the McLintocks' front door and she stood crying. No one went over to her, they were too busy trying to calm

Jeannie down. I wanted to cross the lobby and give her a hug but I was terrified that Jeannie would hit me. Finally, the policewoman noticed Jean and led her back inside. But Jeannie wasn't finished. She was sobbing and still hitting the wall. Then she turned to Arthur.

"And you!! You're never here when I need you. Drinking with him", she pointed to dad, "as our baby was dying. Out all day enjoying yourself and I'm left to run the house and watch the two of them!! You never help. Ever. Now look what's happened!! If you'd been home she'd still be here. You're as bad as they are. I hate you all!" Jeannie pushed Arthur and she ran downstairs. He ran after her. Dad closed our door and led mum into the living room.

"Look, she doesn't know what she's saying. She's hysterical and angry. You just have to ignore it. I know it's going to be hard, but you have to remember that she's lost her child. God alone knows what happened and I suppose we'll find out sooner or later, but for now we have to be strong and let nature run its course. She'll get really angry and blame people. It's natural".
I was confused. My thoughts were jumbled up.

"But dad she said some really horrible things. She shouted at me. And she made mum cry. And Jean was standing there crying as well. I used to like Jeannie but I don't any more. I hate her".

"Hate is too strong a word to use. At the moment Jeannie doesn't know what she's saying. It's called grieving. When you miss someone so much it hurts", dad looked at mum, "don't take this to heart.

Both of you would be the same if someone you cared about and loved died suddenly. Come on now, stop crying".

I nodded. "I felt really sad when twinkle died. I loved granny's cat and I know she was old and couldn't eat much, but when granny said she'd died, I felt really sad. I was angry too. I prayed to God that she'd be well, and he let her die. I felt angry with him for not making her better".

Dad said that was what Jeannie was going through. Only much, much worse and we should be nice to her and understand how she felt.

I didn't want to go to bed. I was scared and upset, but dad said I needed my sleep as next day was a school day. Mum had stopped crying and came through to my bedroom with me. She hugged me tightly.

"Will Jeannie get into our house? What if she tries to?"

"No, the door's locked. No one can come in. Now don't fret about it, just try and get some sleep. School tomorrow". Mum kissed my head. Dad came in and did the same.

I fell asleep after tossing and turning for a while. I hoped Jean would be at school the next day.

CHAPTER 10

I woke up crying and shaking. It was the middle
of the night and dark outside. I was hot and
clammy and my pyjamas were wet and clinging
to me. I had another nightmare. This time I
dreamt that Mary was still alive and living in the
drying shed. She waited for any of us to enter
and then she tried to kiss us. I couldn't see her
face because it was covered by a veil. She kept
pointing to the ghost who sat in the corner. I was
in the shed and I was trying to escape but she
wouldn't let me. I tried to push her away, but she
held my hand tightly and pulled me nearer to the
ghost.

I shouted for mum and she came running into
the bedroom. She had on a blue nightdress and
had brown curlers in her hair.

"It's okay, it's okay. It was just a bad dream.
You're fine. I'm here now. Come on, you're
okay". Mum tried to soothe me, she held me
tightly and stroked my hair but I was really
scared. I couldn't stop crying. She asked what
my dream was about. I told her.

"It's okay, it was just a dream. And I've told
you, there isn't a ghost in the shed. It's just an
old sheet that's been left in there by someone
from another flat. You have too much
imagination".

Dad came through. He had on red and white
stripy pyjamas and his hair was sticking up.
"This is her doing", he nodded towards the door,

"I know what I said earlier, but she's given her", he pointed to me, "nightmares. I think it might be best if you and your mum went to stay with granny for a while. Just until things settle down".

Mum shook her head. "I'm not leaving my house. I haven't done anything wrong. And I'm not sending madam here to live with my mother. We stay here, together".

I could see dad was pleased as he smiled slightly. He didn't really want mum and myself to go. But it was a suggestion.

Mum fetched me a glass of water. She sat with me until I fell asleep again. I felt safe with her there. I didn't want to dream about Mary again. EVER.

CHAPTER 11

I woke up feeling unsettled from the night before. I lay in bed for a while, listening to my mum and dad talking in the kitchen. I could vaguely remember my dream and it still scared me. I didn't want to upset mum though, so I made up my mind to tell her that I was okay if she asked. I heard the front door slam as dad left for his work. I could have gone through to the kitchen, but mum always came in and opened my curtains on a school day, so I lay in bed and waited for her to open my door. I thought about the weekend. It wasn't exactly a terrific one. What with all the arguments Mary had on Saturday morning and afternoon, and then with her missing. I remembered Saturday evening. How Jean and I played and mum and Jeannie sat in the kitchen talking and drinking tea. Then Mary was nowhere to be found. And how Jeannie was upset but very angry with her. And I thought about Arthur shouting and crying, and Jeannie screaming. And then yesterday, Jeannie angry with mum. The weekend had started out just as a normal weekend and then it stopped being nice and ended up horrid.

I lay there trying to remember what Mary looked like. Funny, but I just couldn't picture her. Oh I remembered her hair colour and her nice clothes, but I couldn't remember her face. It was as if she had disappeared. And in a way she had. It was hard to imagine that we would never

99

see her again. That Mary would never be sitting with Anita, by the drying shed ever again. I couldn't even remember her voice. I liked Mary really, but ever since her granny died, she was different. She didn't want to talk to me and she didn't want to play anymore. It was as if a different Mary had come in the night and swapped our nice, funny Mary for a horrid one. I remembered the old Mary who laughed a lot and taught us songs. The one who helped her mum to hang the clothes on the clothesline.

The one who gave us sweets when she had some. I felt funny inside. Like I wanted to cry.

I wasn't sure what was happening to me, but I wanted everything to be back to normal. Back to how it was a year ago when everyone was happy. I wondered if we would ever be like that again.

I was lying there, with my covers pulled up to my neck so I felt nice and cozy, thinking about everything when mum came into the room.

"Oh you're awake. Well the sun is shining but it's not very warm today. I've lit the fire in the living room and your clothes are warming in there. Now quick, come on, run to the bathroom and I'll get your breakfast ready. Quick now". Mum pulled back the curtains.

I ran to the living room where mum had lit the fire and I dressed quickly. After I dressed and tied my shoe laces, I went into the kitchen to have my breakfast. I didn't feel like eating though. I sat and looked at my cereal. Mum noticed and asked what was wrong. She thought it was because of my nightmare. I told her it wasn't.

"Well what's the matter then? Was it because of what went on yesterday? Are you feeling I'll? What is it?"

I replied "No mum it's nothing about yesterday and I'm okay. It's just that I usually walk to school with Jean and I don't suppose she'll be going today. I just feel sad and I want to cry".

Mum hugged me and said she would walk with me if I wanted her to. I said no. I'd be fine. I knew I'd see her at dinner time anyway. Mum was one of the dinner ladies. It felt odd at first, when I went to the academy, to have my mum serving me my dinner. But I soon got used to it. Actually it was nice on one hand because I could talk to her, but on the other hand I knew I had to behave myself because mum would find out what I'd been up to.

So I hugged mum and left to walk to school. I knew a few of the children who lived in nearby tenements.

They went to the Academy as well, and Jean and I sometimes walked with them so I thought I'd meet up with them and tag along.

It was very strange not knocking on the McLintocks' door and asking if Jean was ready. I stopped outside and listened. It was quiet. I felt sad again. Mum must have realised that I was tempted to see how Jean was, because she came into the lobby.

"I knew it!" she said "I knew you'd be

thinking about disturbing them. What have I told you? You just won't take a telling will you? Now get going. Go on! Now!"

I went reluctantly and I dragged my feet as I went? Mum shouted downstairs that I had to walk properly and not scuff my shoes because they cost a lot of money and money didn't grow on trees. So I sulked for a while. I walked downstairs with my head down and I glowered at the steps.

At the entrance to our tenement I met Sally Evans. She lived in the next block. She was in my class at school. Jean didn't like her much because one time Sally told the teacher that Jean was passing notes in class. Jean got into trouble and after school she went over to Sally and shouted at her. They didn't talk after that. I tried to get them to say sorry, but they refused. Sally wanted to know everything about Mary.

"Did you see anything? Someone told my mum that Mary was lying covered in blood. Was she? Did you see her dead body? What did the police say?"

I told her that I hadn't seen anything and I couldn't tell her anything. She was disappointed. She said I wasn't telling her the truth. That I must know what was going on and that I was being spiteful on purpose. I felt like crying but I wanted to hit her at the same time. It suddenly occurred to me that maybe a lot of my class mates might feel the same way.

They would want to talk to me but only to find out what I knew about Mary's death. Sally didn't say anything else to me. We walked in silence and finally got to school. The stone walls and gates seemed huge. The big entrance door was open and I could smell the polish that the cleaners used every evening to keep the wooden floors shining.

I dreaded going into school. I felt sick. Would the teacher know what was going on? Would anything be said at assembly?

We sat in the main hall and the headmaster started our assembly with a hymn. Then he read out some notices and finally we had a prayer. Nothing was mentioned. I was relieved. After assembly, we made our way to the classroom. I sat at my desk. Normally Jean sat next to me. Only, today there was an empty space. Wilma Smith sat behind me. She poked my back and hissed 'Hey!' and passed a note to me.

"Was there a lot of blood?" it read. I looked over my shoulder and shook my head. A few seconds later I received another note.

"What did she look like?"
I didn't look round this time. I just shrugged my shoulders. Again, after a second or two, another note was given to me.

"Was she stabbed? Was there a knife? Was she strangled? How did she die?"
I couldn't take it anymore. I knew that others were dying to ask questions. They kept looking at me and then at Wilma. I heard one of them tell Wilma what to write in a note and then to give it to me. I felt the room closing in on me. My tears started running down my cheeks and I couldn't

stop them. I cried loudly. My shoulders went up and down and I howled. The teacher came over to me.

"Are you okay? Do you want to go for a drink of water and try to calm down?"

I couldn't stop crying. I knew everybody was looking at me, but I couldn't breathe properly and I felt sick and I realised that Mary really was dead. Up until then it had been like a dream. Now it was real.

I don't know what happened after that. Or at least I couldn't remember because everything started spinning then it went dark. Next thing I knew, I was lying on a bed – Well it was a kind of bed -- in the school nurses room and my mum was standing over me.

"Thank goodness you're okay. You scared us all half to death. Would you like a glass of water? Can you sit up? Slowly now", the nurse talked quietly.

Mum looked pale. "I'm taking you home".

I nodded my head. I just wanted to be back home.

Mum walked with her arm round my shoulders. I felt okay, but she said I should walk slowly. She kept asking if I felt dizzy. I didn't. I told her that when I was in the classroom, I kept getting notes from other girls and it made me upset. Mum said she had talked to my teacher Mrs. Dunn, and she said she would tell the other pupils not to bother me. I felt relieved.

When we arrived at the tenement, Mrs. Robertson was coming out carrying her shopping bag. She stopped to ask why I wasn't at school.

"She's had a bad morning. It's a shame, but some pupils were bothering her about what's happened. She just felt bad and needed to come back home", mum turned to me, "but you'll be okay".

I nodded. Mrs. Robertson said that mum needed to take care of me. That it was an awful business and that it affected us all. Then she said that the police had been round asking her questions.

"They asked if I saw anything. I told them that I was at the bingo and didn't get back until after 10 o'clock. It was all over by then I believe. Bunty told them that she and Brian had left around 8 o'clock to go to the cinema. They were late back. They missed the last bus and had to walk the two miles home. Bunty wasn't happy. She had on those new shoes, the high heeled ones, and her feet hurt. They asked if we had seen anything before we left. I told them I left just after 6 o'clock. I went to Meggie's for a cup of tea before we went to bingo. Bunty said it was dark when they left and she heard someone shouting a bit earlier. She thought it was Mr. Milne".

Mum nodded. "Yes, Robbie got out. Apparently the door wasn't locked properly and he ran downstairs. He ran down the back green but Mr. Milne caught up with him, thankfully. I feel sorry for him. If Robbie gets out, and he hasn't for a while, there's no knowing how far he could go".

"I know", Mrs. Robertson tutted, "I remember the time when he ran off and they found him six miles away heading for the beach. The problem is that he's fast. He's gone in the blink of an eye".

I tugged at mums, sleeve. I was desperate to go to the bathroom. Mum said goodbye to Mrs. Robertson and we went upstairs into our flat. I could hear Robbie singing loudly to himself. He wasn't singing his usual 'Humpty Dumpty' though. He was singing 'Mary had a little lamb'. I was glad to be home. Mum made me go to my bedroom and change my clothes. I put on my green t shirt and jeans. I went through to the living room. The fire was lit and I sat on the settee. Mum gave me a blanket to wrap around myself.

"Are you hungry? Would you like a sandwich?" I could tell that mum was worried about me.

I shook my head. "Mum you need to get ready to go to your work. I'm sorry for causing trouble mum".

Mum sat down beside me. "Look, you aren't any trouble. I should have known by the nightmares you've been having, that all of this about Mary has had an effect on you. It's bound to. It's affecting all of us. And don't worry about my work. I've had a word with the head teacher and its fine".

I was pleased. I liked being at home with mum. I wondered what lessons my classmates would be having. I liked school; I always had a good report but I often got into trouble because I talked a lot.

Mum sat with me for a while, then she went through to the kitchen to make a cup of tea. I sat and listened. I could hear footsteps from Mr. Milne's flat above. Robbie was singing and walking around.

Whilst mum was busy in the kitchen, I went into her bedroom and looked out of the window. The policemen were still there. I wondered when we could use the green again. Mum came into the room.

"I thought you'd be in here. It's strange isn't it? No clothes on the line and it being a Monday. I'd usually be out there talking to Mrs. Bruce. It's so quiet. I've never seen this place so still and silent before".

It was strange. We went back into the living room. Mum gave me some paper and I got my crayons and started to draw. I was almost finished drawing a ballerina, when someone knocked at our door. Mum went to answer it and came back followed by a policeman.

"This nice man is going to ask you a few questions. He saw us coming home and thought it might be better to see us both whilst there isn't anyone around". Mum sat on the settee and I joined her. We'd never had a policeman in our flat before. He was tall and had shiny things on his uniform. He had a nice face though. He smiled at me and asked me if I remembered what Mary was like on Saturday.

I told him that she was horrid to me, Jean, Bunty and Robbie. I told him about Peter and Billy and Mrs. Bruce and what she said to Mary. I even told him about the sweets. Then he asked mum a few questions. Mainly about Saturday evening when Jeannie started looking for Mary. It took a long time and I wondered, as he talked to mum, if he knew how Mary had died. I wanted to ask him, but I thought mum might give me into trouble for being nosey again. He was nice but I was relieved when he left. Mum closed the front door and came back into the living room.

"Well at least we've told him everything we know and what went on. I wonder what happened though. It's all very strange. I wonder who the last person to talk to Mary was. Or to see her".

"We should have asked the policeman", I said.

"He wouldn't be able to tell us anything". Mum looked out of the window. "Because the family have to be the first to know. Whatever happened on Saturday night, the family must be told first. It's how the police do things".

Mum turned to me. "I know this is horrible for you. You're stuck inside and you can't play with your friend. You're wondering if you'll ever see her again and what she'll say to you. And I must say, I feel the same. After last night and Jeannie's shouting and carrying on, I wonder if we'll ever be friends again. It upset me and it must have upset you. She shouldn't have done that. But you have to remember that it's the grief making her say these things. The family are in shock. No one could have foreseen what took place on Saturday night. I still can't work it out. It's a mystery right enough".

I knew what mum said was the truth. It scared me but at the same time I was curious. I found it hard to come to terms with Mary dying. It was an odd feeling that I'd never see her again. I felt sad for the family and for my mum who was very upset by Jeannie shouting at her.

CHAPTER 12

What occurred next was something I never expected. Arthur knocked at our door.

"I'm here because I need to apologise for last night. Jeannie didn't know what she was saying. The doctor came over and gave her a strong sedative. She's still asleep".

Mum nodded and stood with her hands on her hips. "Well I must say that I'm surprised to see you here Arthur Mclintock. You upset me, and that was bad enough, but you upset and scared my daughter, and that's unforgiveable. You shouldn't frighten a child like that. She had nightmares and now she's here, at home, because she was so upset that she was crying at school. I accept your apology, and I'm sorry for you, but I don't think that I want to stand here and have a conversation with you".

Arthur looked embarrassed. He shuffled his feet and coughed. "I just wondered if Jean could maybe come over. She's still upset but I wondered if she could just have a short while away from the flat".

I heard everything and went running to the door.

"Mum please let Jean come over, Please mum".

Mum said yes, but only for a short while. I was delighted. Jean could have some paper and draw, just as I was. We could play a game and have some lemonade. I couldn't wait for her to arrive.

Arthur came in with Jean. He thanked mum and told Jean to behave herself. After he left, mum went to get us some lemonade. I was delighted to see her.

"Hey, how are you? Would you like to play a game? I could get out the Ludo or Snakes and Ladders? What would you prefer?"

Jean shrugged. "No thanks. I don't feel like it".

"Well would you like to draw? I've lots of paper. We can share my crayons". I opened the packet.

Again, Jean shrugged. "No I don't want to".

Mum came through with the lemonade. She handed me a glass and turned to give Jean one.

"Here you are. Would you like a biscuit as well?"

Jean shook her head. I was a bit surprised. She never refused a biscuit.

I looked at mum. She shook her head to warn me not to say anything, but I just had to.

"What's wrong with you? Is it because Mary's gone? But that's okay isn't it? You said that you wanted the bedroom to yourself. And you wanted to have your mum and dad to yourself as well. You said that you hated Mary".

Jean burst into tears. Mum wasn't pleased with me. Mum hugged Jean and glared at me. "Just because someone says something, it doesn't mean that they want it to happen. You need to learn how to be tactful and more caring missy!"

Jean sobbed. "I know I said those things, but I just wish Mary was here. I didn't mean them and now she's dead. It's my fault. I wanted her to be gone and now she is".

Mum kept hugging Jean. Finally she cupped Jean's face in her hands and made Jean look at her. "What you said was in the heat of the moment. You really loved your sister and, deep down, she loved you. It wasn't your fault. It wasn't anybody's fault. It happened and that's that. You weren't to blame for anything. Get that out of your mind".

I was confused. Jean had said that she wished Mary was gone. Now she was crying about it. She wasn't the same Jean.

I had expected her to be happy and wanting to play, but she didn't. In fact she didn't want to do anything. She sat by mum and cried and cried. I couldn't think of anything to say to Jean because I didn't want to upset her any more than she was. So I sat at her other side and hugged her as well. After a while she stopped crying. Mum gave her a handkerchief and I kept my arm round her. She wiped her eyes and gave me a half smile.

"I can't help thinking about how Mary and I argued. We seemed to always row; at least for the past few months. But before that, we were friends. I miss her. Even arguing with me. I really miss her".

I nodded. I told Jean about how I missed granny's cat. Mum said it wasn't really the same, but Jean understood what I meant. Mum asked if Jean would like to stay and have lunch. Jean said yes and mum went to make some sandwiches. Jean and I talked. We remembered all the times when Mary played skipping with us. The times we played chase and when it rained, the times we played Ludo in Jeannie's living room. It made us feel a bit sad but happy as well. Jean talked about Marys' books and her collection of foreign dolls. I was worried that she would start crying again but she said that talking about Mary helped. Mum overheard us and as we ate our lunch she told us that sometimes it's better to talk about things that upset us rather than keeping it bottled up inside.

After a while mum took Jean back home. Before she went, I hugged her and I gave her a plastic horse that I got from a lucky bag. She smiled and thanked me by giving me a huge hug. When mum returned, she said it was nice of me to give Jean the toy. I was pleased that I'd done something right.

CHAPTER 13

Monday afternoon dragged by. The sun was shining. It was so inviting that I wanted to go outside. I felt restless; I couldn't sit still and I didn't know what to do with myself but I didn't know why. Having Jean over should have helped but it didn't. She went back home after an hour. I couldn't help but think that the friend I played with on Saturday had gone. Another Jean had taken her place. One that I wasn't sure about. She was serious and sad and seemed older. I couldn't put my finger on it, but there was quite a change in her.

Mum and I went to the local shop. As soon as we entered, the assistant started talking about Mary.

"Hello. What a lovely day. Nippy but at least the sun's shining. You live next door to that girl don't you? Any word about her? Was she murdered like people are saying? Awful business isn't it?"

Mum shook her head. "No we haven't heard anything. I don't think it's nice to be gossiping about it though. The family have enough troubles without people spreading rumours about them".

The assistant wasn't pleased. She gave mum a horrid look. I could tell that she wanted to know more about what happened because she kept asking questions. I was glad to leave the shop. It seemed as if everywhere we went, people would ask about Mary. It made me want to stay in our house. At least I felt safe there.

When dad returned from his work, we sat in the living room and mum told him what had happened at school and at the shop. He folded his arms and shook his head. He said I needed to go to school but I shouldn't have to put up with questions about 'you know who'. Mum told him about Jean. He tutted.

"It's a shame. The problem is people forget about children and how they feel. And poor Jean has to hear Jeannie blaming you and having hysterics. It's not a good atmosphere for the girl".

Mum agreed. Then she went into the kitchen to cook our tea and I went with her. I sat at the table and watched but soon there was a lot of shouting coming from the lobby.

"What in the name of God is going on out there?" Dad got up from his chair in the living room and went towards the front door.
"Don't. Just ignore it. Come on, tea will be ready soon". Mum was worried.

Dad opened the front door. I went and stood behind him. Robbie was being led downstairs by a policeman. He was crying and shouting. Mr. Milne came downstairs behind Robbie, with another policeman. He was talking and waving his arms around. When he saw dad, he looked at him and said very loudly that Robbie was being taken to the police station for questioning. Robbie was very upset, as was Mr. Milne. Dad tried to talk to the policeman with Mr. Milne, but he was told to keep out of the way. Arthur Mclintock heard the noise and came out of the flat. He saw what was going on and started to shout at Mr. Milne.

"I hope he rots in hell. He killed my little girl. He'll get his reward in hell".

Dad asked Arthur what he was talking about. Arthur had tears in his eyes.

"The police say that Mary had a wound on her head and marks on her cheek. It looks like she was struck and fell. They think she might have hit her head on the stool". Arthur started sobbing. "Someone must have pushed her. They left her there. They left my little girl there to die alone on the cold floor. My Mary!"

Arthur couldn't say anything else, he was crying hysterically. The policewoman who was staying with the McLintocks came out.

She took his arm and said "That's enough. Come on now. Come on". She led him back inside and closed the door.

Dad gulped. Mum had joined us to see what was going on. The shouting had continued.

By now both Robbie and Mr. Milne were outside. When mum heard what Arthur was saying, she put her hand over her mouth.

"Oh, dear God. That poor girl. And she was still alive? Would the person who hit her have known that?"

Mum was shaking. Dad held her arm and took mum inside. I was scared and shut the door. We all sat in the living room. Dad spoke first.

"So now we know. Mary was struck on her

116

cheek, fell backwards and hit her head. Then whoever was there, covered her over with a sheet. I wonder if they did know that she was alive? Whoever it was, must have panicked".

Mum nodded. "Well no doubt the police will find out sooner or later but I just can't see it being Robbie. Oh I know he has tantrums and shouts. Sometimes he lashes out at people, usually Mr. Milne. But I don't see him doing anything like hitting Mary then covering her over. His mind doesn't work like that. I wonder what'll happen. I bet Bunty will be upset, with Robbie being questioned and all".

Dad agreed. "Oh well, no use trying to work it out. Come on, let's just forget about it for now. Will tea be ready soon?" Dad looked at me, "I don't know about you, but I'm feeling a bit hungry".

We ate our tea in silence. I was thinking about school next day.

I could imagine the others asking me about Robbie and saying that he'd killed Mary. I didn't want to go. I felt a bit sick. Mum noticed that I was quieter than usual.

"What's the matter? Are you brooding about Mary? Or are you upset about Robbie having to go to the police station? Come on, tell me what the matter is. And stop playing with your food".

I put my fork down. "I don't want to go to school and have everybody asking questions again. It's horrible. I wish we lived in another street. Or another town. I hate all of this. I wish we were away from here!"

Dad stopped eating. "Well we don't. This is our home whether you like it or not. What's happened is sad, but there are times in our lives when awful things happen. You just have to take a deep breath and get on with life. You need to go to school. You can't fall behind with your work. Now eat your tea. Mum made this and it's rude of you not to have any. Food isn't for playing with, there are starving children around the world who would be glad to eat your food. Stop this nonsense and eat up".

I really didn't want to eat anything, but dad was annoyed with me so even though I felt as if I would be sick, I ate it all.

After tea, we sat in the living room. Mum tried to read her magazine, the one she had on Saturday but wasn't able to read because of Mary. I drew pictures and dad read his paper then someone knocked at our door. Mum went to answer it. We heard voices in the hallway and mum came into the living room followed by Mrs. Bruce.

"Hello, I've just come up to see if there's any news about Mary. I was sitting in my living room, minding my own business, when I heard an awful row outside. Shouting and wailing. Awful it was. So I looked out and you'll never guess. Robbie was being put into a police car. Mr. Milne went in it as well.

Why have they been taken by the police? I asked myself. Well, I don't mind telling you, I always knew there was something fishy about those people". She hardly took a breath as she said this to mum.

Dad put his paper down. "I believe that the police are just asking Robbie some questions. No one's been charged as far as I know. It's best not to speculate. We'll be told what's happening all in good time".

Mrs. Bruce was having none of it. "Well I've seen that Robbie when he's gone into a tantrum. Scary it is. He throws himself around and screams blue murder. Then he lashes out at whoever's nearest. I'm telling you, he shouldn't be in the tenement. He should have been locked up years ago. He's not safe to be around".

I could see mum was beginning to lose her temper. She smiled, but it didn't reach her eyes.

"Robbie is harmless. Mr. Milne looks after him really well. And Bunty often helps him. If he was so bad, she wouldn't go near the place. I feel sorry for Mr. Milne. He spends all his time trying to keep Robbie happy and out of any trouble. Yes Robbie can be a handful, but I'm sure he would never hurt anyone on purpose".

Mrs. Bruce turned and went into the hallway.

"Well I just think it's strange how the police have taken that lad away. That's all I'm saying".

Mum just said that we had to wait and see and not spread gossip. Mrs. Bruce wasn't happy. Dad shook his head and went back to reading the paper. I followed mum into the hall. Mrs. Bruce looked at me.

"Before I go, I heard that you had a bad time at school. What was wrong? Were you ill?"

Mum stepped in. "No she's just tired and needs

some rest. Goodbye".

Mrs. Bruce left in a huff. We watched her going downstairs. I was glad she'd gone. She was really nosey. She always wanted to know everybody's business.

As we were about to close the door, Mr. Strachan and Alex came down the stairs. I didn't know that they were upstairs. They didn't look happy. In fact, Mr. Strachan looked very serious.

"Hello, we were upstairs finishing the painting. We heard all the noise. What a carry on".

Mum nodded. "The police have taken Robbie for questioning about Mary's death. Mr. Milne's gone with him. We heard the noise as well. I hope there'll be some news soon".

Mr. Strachan looked at us. He seemed sad.

"When the council said we'd been given the flat, we were over the moon. Our house is condemned and we thought we'd have to move to another area. As it happens, that might have been a good idea. My wife is terrified to come over here. What with all that's happened its set her right off. She's bothered with her nerves and she just can't handle any kind of upset. This weekend has been very upsetting for her. You can imagine how she feels. Well we're going to have to think twice about moving here. You just never know who's living next to you and with what happened in this tenement building, it's now obvious that there's a killer on the loose. I have to admit, I had second thoughts about being here today".

Mum didn't know what to say. I could see she was annoyed but also sad. So I spoke.

"We like living here. It's nice. The people are nice and everybody helps you when you've a problem. Robbie hasn't done anything. I know he can be strange, but he's okay really".

Mum found her voice. "She's right. This has been a great place to live. We like everyone. It's upsetting for us all to think someone could have had a hand in Mary's death, but there's never been any other trouble here. We have a super community. If you decide not to move, then it'll be your loss".

Alex answered. "Mary was a strange girl wasn't she. She was very pretty but when you took that away, she wasn't nice at all.

She seemed to love teasing people. She never knew when to stop though".

I knew what he meant. But he was wrong. Mum spoke up. "Mary was confused that's all. She had a bad start to the day and took it out on others. Deep down she was a nice enough child. But you'll never see that now. Everyone who knew her, knew the real Mary. It's a shame you saw the ugly side of her, a real shame".

Mr. Strachan didn't say anything for a minute or two. Then he turned to Alex. "Come on we'd better get a move on. Your mother will be wondering where we are", he looked at us, "perhaps we'll see you later. Goodbye for now". And with that, they left.

We went inside and told dad what Mr. Strachan said. Dad said that it might be best that the Strachans' didn't move in. He said it was bad enough having Mrs. Bruce and all her dramatics in the tenement without another hysterical woman moving in. Mum tutted but said she had to agree.

The rest of the evening went quietly. No shouting or screaming in the lobby. But we knew that Robbie and Mr. Milne weren't home because we hadn't heard them coming back. We always heard Robbie. He sang most of the time and it echoed in the lobby. Mum was worried about them. She wondered how they were getting on. She mentioned them a few times. Dad said there was no use in getting worked up about it.

The police had a job to do and one way or another they'd find out what happened to Mary. I was more concerned about going to school next day.

I knew my class mates wouldn't give up asking me questions as they were nosey. I told mum how I felt. She said that she'd go into school with me and have another talk with the teachers because she didn't want a repeat of the mornings' shenanigans. I wasn't convinced but I thought it was best to put on a brave face. Mum wouldn't be worried if she thought that I was okay. Dad always said that mum worried if she had nothing to worry about. Everything worried her, it was her nature.

I went to bed still thinking about school. The drama of the day hadn't helped. Was Robbie involved in some way? And would Mrs.

Strachan move into Mrs. McNab's flat. Everything was jumbled and, as I fell asleep I hoped that the next day would be better.

CHAPTER 14

Mum came into my bedroom and opened the curtains. I hadn't slept too well. I spent a long time trying to get comfortable. I just couldn't get to sleep. My thoughts kept me awake so, when mum asked if I had a good night's sleep, I lied and said yes. I didn't want to upset her any more than she already was. Everything was wrong. When I had eventually fallen asleep, I was chewing some gum I found in the drawer of my bedside table. Now I had gum stuck in my hair. Mum went mad. She couldn't brush my hair properly and had to cut the gum out. I cried. Mum said it was my own fault. Then I spilled milk over the table. And I couldn't find my pencil case. It was a bad start to the day. Mum was rushing around.

"Come on, hurry up. I need to go to the shop after I've been to your school. Quick now, where's your coat?"
I could have sworn that my coat was hanging in the hallway. It wasn't. I don't know how it ended up in my bedroom. Mum wasn't amused.

"Come on, we haven't got all day". Mum wanted to leave.

I wasn't really dawdling, I just didn't want to go to school. I thought it would be easier to be at home. However, mum was determined and said "You are going whether you like it or not".

So we left I couldn't help grumbling. I dragged my feet and stared at the ground.

As mum locked the door, the policeman who stayed overnight with the McLintocks came out of their flat. He nodded to us and followed us down the stairs. Mum didn't say anything. I wanted her to ask him about Robbie but decided it was best to remain silent. As we approached the front step of the tenement, Bunty came out of her flat. She smiled at us.

"Hello. Off to school then?" she looked at me. Mum nodded. "Yes I'm going in with her. She had a bad day yesterday. The crying at school and then what went on in the lobby honestly it was quite a day".

"Oh dear" Bunty looked at me "I hope you're okay now", she turned to mum, "Why? What went on yesterday? I was at work until six o'clock. When I came back everything was quiet".

Mum told her about Robbie being questioned and Mr. Milne going with him.

"I hope they let Robbie go. If he had anything to do with Marys' death, I expect he'll be taken away somewhere. We might never see him again. Poor Mr. Milne was in quite a state. Robbie was shouting and screaming. I thought the police would maybe ask him a few questions and then let him come back home. But no. As far as I can tell he's still at the police station".

Bunty's face drained of all colour. She was shaking and she shouted.

"Oh god. Oh god no! But they can't lock Robbie up. Oh no!"

We were startled. I didn't like how Bunty was

shouting and I hid behind mum. Mum folded her arms across her chest and looked across at the policeman. Bunty kept saying no and shouted louder and louder. The policeman had come over beside us and was watching her. Mrs. Robertson heard Bunty shouting and came out.

"What's going on?" Mrs. Robertson tried to talk to Bunty. "Why are you shouting? What's the matter with you?"

Bunty looked at her mum. "I'm so sorry. I'm sorry mum. I didn't mean it. It was an accident. It just happened".

Mrs. Robertson was confused. "What was an accident? What happened? What are you talking about?"

Bunty started to cry. Great gulping sobs. It was scary. Mum put her arm round Bunty's shoulder.

"Come on, it's okay I'm sure they'll let Robbie go soon".

Bunty shook her head. She looked at her mother who was standing beside her trying to understand what was wrong. The policeman walked over and stood next to me.

"Mum it was an accident". Bunty went on through her tears. "I didn't mean it. She was there when I went to get my clothes. She started to make fun of my locket and my ring. Then she said Brian preferred her and she'd take him away from me".

Mrs. Robertson still hadn't figured out what Bunty was saying.

"Who? What are you talking about? Bunty

what are you saying?"

Mum knew. She talked quietly to Bunty.

"Are you sure you want to tell us this?"

Bunty nodded. "I've felt sick with worry all weekend. When she started saying things, I couldn't help it. I lost my temper and hit her. Just here." She pointed to her cheek. "She said she was going to get the police. She said she'd tell them that I hit her and I'd lose my job and Brian. I pushed her and she fell over." Bunty sobbed louder "I didn't mean it. Honestly". She looked at the policeman. "She fell and hit her head on the stool. Then she lay there making a gurgling noise. I didn't know what to do. I panicked. I covered her with the old sheet that was in the corner".

The policeman shook his head. He talked to Mrs. Robertson.

"Can you take her inside. I need to go and get another policeman. We need a statement. She'll be taken to the station".

Mrs. Robertson was crying. "Oh Bunty, Bunty. What have you done? And all because a stupid little girl got to you. I told you before, she was bad news. Now look at the mess you're in!"

Bunty sobbed. "Brian came round before I could get help. I was scared to tell him. We went to the cinema but I couldn't concentrate. I was going to tell you when we got back.

Then I saw all the police and I couldn't bring myself to say anything. When I heard Arthur shouting and Jeannie screaming, well it was awful. I knew that Mary was dead. I shouldn't have pushed her, but I did. And now she's dead".

The policeman took Bunty's arm and led her inside. Mrs. Robertson followed. Mum looked at me.

"Well at least we know what happened now. It was an accident. Poor Bunty and poor Mary".

"What will happen to Bunty now?" I was curious, "will Robbie come back home?"

Mum shrugged. "I don't know what'll happen to Bunty. It was an accident after all. Yes I expect Robbie will be back soon. Come on, I think we can keep you at home today. Let's go back upstairs. After all this excitement, I don't know about you, but I need a cup of tea".

I agreed. It was all very odd and upsetting but I was glad it was over. And I wouldn't have to go to school. Hurrah!

EPILOGUE

Mary's funeral took place two weeks after her death. Usually coffins were taken into the house and put in the bedroom. People would visit and pay their respects to the family and the dead. However, the McLintocks didn't want this. Jeannie didn't want to see her child lying cold in a box my mum said. She didn't want young Jean to have the last image of her sister as a corpse. So, it was decided that Mary would be in her coffin at Davidson's funeral parlour which was three streets away. Neither my mum nor dad went to see her although plenty of others did. My dad said they were either nosey or ghoulish. They just wanted something to gossip about and they didn't take into account the feelings of the family. Mrs. Bruce from the tenement went to view her.

"It was so sad. She looked beautiful. Just like she was asleep. Pink oyster satin lining and a lovely lace collar. What a shame. What a sore heart that family must have. Poor girl. So young with her whole life ahead of her. I have to admit, I shed a tear or two".

I wondered why she had changed her tune. Only two weeks before, Mrs. Bruce had called Mary a troublemaker, a horrible child and said that she needed to watch her step. Just because Mary was dead, was it right that people thought she was lovely and nice? I remembered how horrid she was to us all. The arguments and teasing. Oh yes, part of me was sad that she was dead, but another part was relieved that we wouldn't have to run the gauntlet of her taunts and nastiness any more. I figured that Jean would be relieved as well. She could sleep okay now without being scared at what Mary might do to her. I said this to my mum. She was horrified.

"You shouldn't speak ill of the dead. No matter how awful she was, Mary didn't deserve to die as she did. Don't ever talk like that again".

After the funeral my dad came home and hugged me tightly. Mum didn't go. She sat in the living room with me and we played a few games of Ludo. I knew she was upset though. She kept going to the kitchen and I heard her crying.

I hadn't seen Jean since the time she came over to play for an hour and then Mrs. Mclintock had a row with mum. I really wanted to knock on her door and talk to her but mum said I shouldn't bother the family. Their flat was quiet. I stopped at the door and listened a few times but I couldn't hear a thing. None of the other children from the tenements went out to play in the drying green.

There was an odd feeling. Like everything was the same on the surface but underneath everything had changed. No one smiled. Even Mr. Milne and Robbie were quiet.

Mrs. Robertson moved from her flat. A lorry came one day and loaded all her furniture and things then the driver locked the door. Dad said she'd gone to live with relatives. Bunty was arrested and sent to prison for a while. People said some awful things but dad said it was an accident and they shouldn't be too hard on her. Brian left soon after Mrs. Robertson and we never heard from any of them again.

Three weeks after Mary's funeral, the Mclintocks moved. It was a Friday and I returned from school happy that the weekend had arrived. A lorry was parked in front of the tenement. I ran upstairs and almost knocked over a man carrying a chair.

"Mind out miss". He shouted at me. I hadn't a clue as to what was going on. I went into our flat and mum was sitting in the kitchen drinking a cup of tea.

"The Mclintocks' are leaving. They can't stay here. Everything reminds them of Mary and each time they go out, people point and whisper at them. Every day, when she looks out of the bedroom window, Jeannie sees the drying shed where Mary died.

They're moving down south to Arthurs' brothers' place until they get a place of their own".

I was shocked. I hadn't seen or talked to Jean for ages. She was my best friend and now she was moving away. I was upset. Before mum could stop me, I ran out of our flat and knocked on the Mclintocks' door.

"Jean, Jean, are you in there? Come out I want to talk to you". I was crying.

A removal man came out.

"Sorry love. The family left two hours ago. I

can't help you. Don't cry. Go home now, go on home".

I went back to our flat and ran to mum.

"I didn't get a chance to see her. I didn't get to say goodbye. It's not fair. Why do they have to leave? I hate Mary, I hate her!"

Mum shook her head.

"It's done now. You've other pals. Life goes on. When you're older you'll understand. Now go and get changed. We'll go out to the shop. I'll get you an ice cream".

And that was that. I never did see Jean again.

We moved a year later. Granny died and left us her house. It had a small garden, a shed and my dad grew vegetables and some flowers for mum. We had no reason to go back to the tenement. Mr. Milne and Robbie lived there for a few more months but when Robbie took ill and died suddenly, Mr. Milne moved away. Mrs. Bruce was the only one who stayed there. Mum never went to see her because she said Mrs. Bruce was a busybody and only gossiped about awful things. The Strachans didn't move into the flat. We didn't see them after that weekend.

Now as I stand here watching the tenement being demolished, I feel a sense of sadness but also relief. The ghosts from the past have gone and as my mum said, life goes on. But I will never forget that weekend. The weekend...

When Mary Died

Dear Reader

If you have enjoyed reading my book then please tell your friends and relatives and leave a review on Amazon.
Thank you.
CL Bell

About the Author

The author was born and brought up in
Peterhead in North East of Scotland. She shares
her Suffolk home with her husband and 5 cats.
She likes the countryside, trees and cake.

If you would like to know more about C.L. Bell
and to follow her on social media please go to

Facebook: C-L-Bell-Author

Twitter: corneliabell

Instagram: belcornelia

Printed in Great Britain
by Amazon